DURARARA!!

1

RYOHGO NARITA

ILLUSTRATION BY **SUZUHITO YASUDA**

VOLUME 1

Ryohgo Narita
ILLUSTRATION BY **Suzuhito Yasuda**

NEW YORK

DURARARA!!, Volume 1
RYOHGO NARITA,
ILLUSTRATION BY SUZUHITO YASUDA

Translation by Stephen Paul

DURARARA!!
© RYOHGO NARITA 2004
All rights reserved.
Edited by ASCII MEDIA WORKS
First published in 2004 by KADOKAWA
CORPORATION, Tokyo.
English translation rights arranged with
KADOKAWA CORPORATION, Tokyo, through
Tuttle-Mori Agency, Inc., Tokyo.

Yen On
Hachette Book Group
1290 Avenue of the Americas
New York, NY 10104
www.hachettebookgroup.com
www.yenpress.com

Yen On is an imprint of Hachette Book Group, Inc.
The Yen On name and logo are trademarks of Hachette Book
Group, Inc.

First Yen On edition: July 2015

ISBN: 978-0-316-30474-0

10 9 8 7 6 5 4 3 2 1

RRD-C

Printed in the United States of America

Prologue

This is a twisted story.

"Hey! Hey! Hey! I know you're in there, Seiji! I'm here again today! Oh no, you forgot to unlock the door! How am I supposed to get inside?"

Warning, warning. My house is under siege by a stalker. She's been pounding on my door for minutes. Why hasn't she thought to try the intercom?

"The door is locked! Are you asleep? Omigosh! How cheeky am I? Sneaking in on a man while he's in bed!"

Alert, alert. Alert to myself last week. Some girls that just moved to the big city were being harassed by a thug, and I saved them from trouble. It turned out they were about to start at the same high school as me tomorrow. And somehow it turned into this. The other girl was so polite and normal, too.

"Hey, I want to tell you something... I just wanted to say, I've been in love with you for a long time! Do you remember me?! I was the girl sitting right next to you during our exams! The boy on my right had this crazy name like Ryuugamine, so I started wondering what the boy on my left was named. And when I turned, it was love at first sight! So I made sure to learn and memorize your name! But I didn't have the guts to speak to you...and then you saved me, and I thought—oh! This must be fate at work! It gave me so much courage! Please, just show me your beautiful face, let me see you looking bright and healthy, please, please, please!"

Caution, caution. She freakin' followed me home. Ever since then, this has happened every day. She doesn't listen when I order her to leave. I've heard these same lines two thousand times.

"Are you not feeling well?! So that's why you're not answering the door! Oh no! You need to open up right away! I've done lots of research since the exam day! I know your birthday, your family members, your—"

Police, police. I'm going to call the cops. Only that threat was enough to finally chase her away.

Three hours after the assault, I felt safe in assuming that she'd finally gone, and I left to pick up some things from the convenience store below my apartment building. Even as I selected my toothpaste and magazines, that stalker chick's face was floating through my brain.

My first impression was that she was gorgeous. There was an adult air to her—she seemed to be a perfect example of a lovely young lady. But personal experience soon taught me exactly how a girl like her could be single.

No amount of good looks made a crazy chick like her palatable. Maybe it was different if you were looking for that—but I wasn't. I already *had* a girlfriend.

So, what to do about the first day of school tomorrow, I wondered as I climbed the stairs to my floor and headed down the narrow hallway.

If I have to meet her there every day, it's better not to go at all. I mean, I've already got a girlfriend. A quiet and graceful one, not like her. As long as I've got my girl, I don't need to bother with high school at all. I could get a part-time job at my sister's company instead.

Oh, now I remember. I was wondering why I even saved that chick in the first place. It's because, at a glance, she looked like my girlfriend—until she opened her mouth. That's why I saved her. It was a stupid decision. I saved her because they looked alike, but she couldn't have been more different on the inside.

I put the key in the lock of my apartment door.

Huh? Weird.

It's already unlocked.

*　　*　　*

Mayday, Mayday, Mayday. My danger sense is on full alert.

Alarm, alarm, beepedy-beep. Inside the door, a pair of women's shoes.

"S-Seiji..."
Farther into my apartment, the stalker was standing stock-still.
I realized that I was taking the presence of this trespassing intruder with remarkable calm. I'd spotted the look on her face.
When I spoke, even I was surprised by the coldness of my voice.

"You *saw*?"

"I, um, er..."
There was terror and unease on her face, nothing like her typical expression.
...Well, well, you're capable of looking like this after all.
That's when I knew she had *seen something she shouldn't have.*
"Uh—um, Seiji, I...I won't tell anyone! This doesn't change how I feel about you. It's okay, I don't care about what you're secretly into. I can change myself to match your interests, just, um..."
The tables have turned. Now I'm the one putting pressure on her.
"It doesn't matter."
"Oh, Seiji!" Her voice filled with hope.
"It doesn't matter."
"Sei...ji?"
She noticed the chill in my eyes, and the hope instantly turned to fear.
I had to take it one step further into absolute despair. I repeated myself.
"It doesn't matter."

"Seiji!"
When my sister burst into the room with two of her employees, I was seated in the living room, eating a cup of instant ramen. The

employees quickly and expertly packed the stalker into a body bag and removed her from the room. My sister made a brief inspection of the place, noted the blood spatter on the wall, then hugged me from behind.

"It'll be all right. You'll be fine."

Her comforting warmth enveloped me. All I thought was that this made it hard to eat.

"There's nothing to worry about, Seiji. Just leave this all to me. Okay?"

"Sis, as for *her*—not the girl, I mean…"

"You were the one who took her out, weren't you? Don't worry, leave all that to me. Understand? As long as I'm here, nothing bad will happen to you… Especially not the police—they won't get you. They'll never get you, so don't worry about that."

And with that, she gave her employees more orders and left.

Maybe it's not the best idea to get a job with her company. She knows a lot of people working in unsavory occupations, people the office doesn't know about. Those men that came in with her took a dead body and did their jobs without a word. They couldn't have been ordinary, law-abiding folks.

I'd rather not work with evil people. They'd turn me evil, too.

If I turned bad and got caught by the police, my girlfriend would be so sad. That's the last thing I want.

I watched the workers calmly scrub the blood off the wall and shoveled more cold, stale ramen into my gullet.

God, this ramen is terrible.

This is a twisted, twisted tale.
A tale of twisted love.

Shadow

Chapter 1

Chat room (weekend, evening)

《I'm telling you, Ikebukuro's all about the Dollars right now!》
[The Dollars are that team people are talking about these days? I've never seen them.]
《Sounds like they're keeping it on the DL in public. But people on the Net are all into it!》
【Oh, really? Sounds like you know a lot about Ikebukuro, Kanra.】
《Not that much really!》
《Oh, how about this? Have you ever heard of the Black Rider?》
【Black Rider?】
[Ahh.]
《The one people are talking about in Shinjuku and Ikebukuro. It was even in the news yesterday.》

♂♀

Location in Bunkyo Ward, Tokyo (weekday, late night)

"Muh...muh...monsterrrrr!"
 The man screamed in rage, lifted his metal pipe—and *ran for his life.*

*   *   *

The man dashed through the late-night parking garage. In his right hand, the pipe was not cold, but skin temperature. Even that sensation became indistinct and uncertain as sweat flooded his palm.

There were no people around, only cars waiting patiently for their owners.

All sound had vanished from around him, leaving only the pounding of his footsteps, his ragged breath, and the steadily rising drumbeat of his heart.

As he tore past the ugly concrete pillars, the thug practically shouted under his breath, "Sh-sh-sh-shit! Shit! Shit! S-s-s-s-screw this, man!"

The light in his eyes took on a glint of anger, but the only breath that escaped his mouth was the panting of sheer terror.

He'd gotten that neck tattoo to inspire fear in others. Now that tattoo was distorted with the tension of his own fear. Soon the purplish pattern, devoid of any kind of belief or meaning, was covered by a pitch-black boot.

♂♀

《It's been around as an urban legend for years, but now that all the cell phones have cameras, people have started getting shots of the Rider, and the story's famous again.》

[Oh yeah, I've heard about that. Actually, it's not even an urban legend, but a regular old motorcycle gangster. Just not the kind that rides in an actual gang.]

《Anyone riding around on two wheels without their lights on has to be an idiot.》

《Assuming they're human.》

[I'm afraid I don't see your meaning.]

《Oh well... I'm saying the Rider's basically a monster!》

♂♀

With an eerie *crikkle* sound, the thug's body flew through the air at an odd angle, half rotating.

Slammed hard sideways, he desperately scrabbled with what remained of his wits. The air was freezing, but the numbness throughout his body shut out the chill of the concrete. Trapped in a nightmare, he turned back to the approaching source of his terror.

The shadow of a figure stood over him. Not metaphorically, either—it was a shadow.

The figure was dressed in a black full-body riding suit without a single pattern or logo on it, making it look as though the black material had been dipped into even darker ink. Only the reflection of the parking garage lights signified that there was even something physical there at all.

From the neck upward was even stranger. An oddly designed helmet sat atop the figure's neck. In comparison to the uniform blackness of the body, the shape and patterning of the helmet seemed somehow artistic. It didn't clash with the overall dark look, however.

The faceplate of the helmet was like the dark mirrored glass of a luxury car. It showed nothing of what lay behind the glass, only the distorted reflection of the lights overhead.

"..."

The shadow was completely silent. It exuded no signs of life whatsoever. The man's face twisted with fear and hatred.

"I-I-I didn't do nothin' to deserve gettin' chased by a T-t-t-terminator!"

It might have passed as a one-liner, but there was no humor in his expression.

"Wh-wh-why don't you say something? What's your problem? What the hell are you?!"

From his perspective, the figure was incomprehensible. They were supposed to meet up in the underground parking garage like usual, do an easy job, then leave. Deliver the product to the client and load up on a new product. That was it. Nothing different from the usual. Where did they screw up? What had they done to call such a monster down upon themselves?

The man and his "colleagues" were supposed to do their ordinary job tonight.

But that ordinary plan had crumbled into dust without warning.

They were standing at the entrance to the garage, waiting for one late straggler, when the thing appeared out of nowhere. A single motorcycle passed by the entrance without a sound, stopping a few dozen feet ahead.

The man and his companions noticed a number of anomalies with this scene.

First, the absolutely silent entrance. Perhaps there had been some slight screeching of the tires on the ground, but the engine itself did not make a sound. Maybe it had been turned off so the motorcycle could coast in silence, but they would have heard the approach of the engine before that, and no one noticed a thing prior to its appearance.

Second, the bike was completely pitch-black, including its rider. That included the engine, driveshaft, and the wheels inside the tires. It had no headlight, and even the place where a license plate would go was just a flat black surface. It was only the reflections of the streetlights and moonlight that helped them recognize it as a motorcycle at all.

But creepiest of all was the large object dangling from the rider's obsidian hand. It was nearly the size of the rider itself, and an opaque liquid dripped from its narrowed end onto the asphalt.

"Koji...?"

One of the man's coworkers recognized what the ragged object was. At the same time, the riding suit astride the bike dropped it—no, *him*—onto the ground.

It was another of their colleagues, the one who'd been late to show up. His face was puffy and beaten, and blood poured from his nose and mouth.

"Are you serious?"

"What the hell?"

The scene was eerie, but none of them felt fear at this point. Neither did they feel any anger about the beating of their companion, Koji. Nothing more than work circumstances united the men, and none of them felt a particular kinship for the others.

"What, huh? Whatchu want?"

A man in a parka, the stupidest of the group, took a step toward the motorcycle. One of them, five of us. The superiority of numbers inflated his attitude a level or two. But the closer he got to the bike, the more his advantage evaporated from five on one to one-on-one. Only the black shadow atop the bike noticed this.

"..."

Jrshk.

A nasty sound. A very, very nasty sound. It transcended simple displeasure and signaled danger to the animal instincts at a fundamental level.

The man in the parka slumped to his knees, then landed on the asphalt face-first.

"Wha...?"

Now the men were unnerved, and their tension spread outward, as it usually did when they were in the middle of their work. All that they were able to ascertain was the presence of the bike before them—there were no other figures nearby. And the shadow atop the vehicle was now stepping down off the bike, its thick black boot hitting the ground.

They saw it being lowered. But the fact that it was lowered meant the foot had been raised in the air before that action. And those with better eyesight noticed something else at the same time.

Tangled into the underside of the descending boot was a pair of glasses belonging to the man in the parka.

This information instantly identified the situation to them.

The man in the parka had been dropped instantaneously with a single kick, delivered while the figure still sat on the bike.

If they'd seen his face, they would see that his nose was twisted and broken. The shadow on the motorcycle had kicked out at a range just long enough not to knock the man backward, catching and breaking his nose in the indentations on the sole of the boot.

But the men watching had no way of realizing this. Half of them wondered how a man kicked in the face ended up falling forward, while the other half ignored it and pulled out police batons or stun guns from their belts.

"Wait...how did that work? Huh? I mean...how...?"

Two colleagues raced past the confused man, roaring with anger as they charged the rider.

"Uh, hey—" he tried to call out as the shadow silently stepped off the bike. It strode over without a change in expression or sound, aside from the crunching of the glasses beneath the boot. The movement was smooth and elegant, as though a shadow had actually been fleshed out into human form.

What happened next was etched into the man's memory in slow motion—either because the events were simply too bizarre not to leave an impression or because the danger of the situation had sped up his concentration so that everything seemed slower.

One of his colleagues pressed his Taser against the shadow.

Wait, does a leather jacket conduct electricity or not? he wondered. The entire shadow twitched and convulsed. Apparently it did. The ordeal was over.

His colleague pressed the stun gun in farther, but in the next moment, his relief evaporated.

Even as the shadow convulsed with electricity, it reached out to the man with the police club and grabbed his arm.

"Wabya—!"

The man with the club, standing on the opposite side of the crackling shadow, grunted and shook violently, then fell to the ground in shock.

"Oh, you're gonna get—"

The man with the Taser noticed the shadow's hand reaching for him now, and he hastily switched off the power. This did not improve his situation—the shadow's powerful wrist seized his neck.

He flailed his limbs desperately, but the shadow's grip remained firm. His feet kicked out at the shins and crotch of his assailant, but the helmet produced nothing but silence and darkness.

"Kah...kuah..."

Strangled until his eyes rolled back into his head, the man with the Taser fell to the ground, joining the one with the police baton.

Shit. Whatever the hell is happening, it ain't good. I haven't done a thing, and now four of the six of us are down, including Koji. Fear began to paint the thug's mind, the indescribable thing overriding any thoughts of his own helplessness.

"You pullin' some kinda MMA crap?"

The other man on the right was calm and cool.

"Gassan!" the thug called out, desperate for any source of strength he could find. The man named Gassan, leader of the coworkers, stoically watched the shadow. There was no terror in his eyes, but neither was there any confidence.

Gassan pulled a large knife out of his jacket and lazily approached the shadow. Careful to watch for any movement, he tried lobbing an insult.

"I dunno where you learned what you're doin'...but you'll still die if I stab you."

He spun the knife in his hand. It wasn't as small as a fruit knife, but it also wasn't the kind of short sword you'd see in a comic book. The handle was just long enough to fit in a palm, and the blade itself was about the same length, sharp edge gleaming.

"And just because you know some martial arts don't mean you can ice me with your bare han— *Aaah!*"

The shadow abruptly interrupted his challenge. It leaned forward slightly, picking up two objects lying on the ground—the police baton and stun gun his colleagues had been using.

"…"

"…"

Stun gun in the right hand, club in the left. It sure was a nasty-looking double-sword stance.

For an instant, the already eerie quiet surrounding the parking garage turned to absolute silence. It was broken by the leader's questioning grumble.

"Wait…you kidding? I thought you were gonna use your kung fu on me."

The words were lighthearted and jocular, but the voice itself was thick with tension and unease. They should have just ganged up on the thing all at once, but it was too late to turn back now.

The thug in the rear couldn't move a step. If this was some other gang or the police, he'd have leaped in to help without hesitation. The four of them would have all jumped the target at once.

But the thing before them was too eerie and otherworldly for that. Their nerves weren't ready to react in the usual way. It was just a human being wearing a riding suit. But the atmosphere surrounding it was so creepy, so alien, that he couldn't help but feel that he'd been sucked into some alternate universe.

Aware of the thug's unease or not, the leader ground his teeth and rolled his tongue.

"You're fightin' dirty! All I got is a knife! Ain't you ashamed of yourself?!"

The shadow turned to the leader, responding to his pointless question with silence.

In the next moment, the thug saw something take clear shape.

♂♀

《So the one riding the black motorcycle isn't a human at all.》
【What is it, then?】

[Just an idiot.]

《Dotachin says it's a Reaper.》

【Dotachin?】

《As a matter of fact, I've seen the black motorcycle chasing someone around.》

【Who's Dotachin?】

[Did you tell the police?]

《I dunno, given what it was carrying, it was already pretty abnormal.》

【…Am I being ignored? Who's Dotachin?!】

《I couldn't tell at first, but the body was making》

【…】

【?】

【Kanra? What happened?】

[I think he got disconnected.]

【What?! But he was in the middle of the story! What came out of the body?!】

【And who is Dotachin?!】

♂♀

"…?"

The shadow began to move strangely as the thug and his boss watched.

It reached down to pick up the stun gun, then placed it on the seat of the bike.

I guess it must be too difficult to use two weapons at once, the thug decided. In the next moment, the shadow gripped the special police club with both hands.

And *twisted* it.

"Wha—?!"

At this, the two men could not contain their shock, and they shared a look. What kind of sleight of hand could possibly bend a police baton like that? If anything, the shadow's frame was slender, not the kind of body that suggested feats of great strength.

In any case, the shadow had now given up the weapons it had just gained—but rather than providing relief to the men, they were even more confused. The level floor of reality that moored their minds was being removed.

Now that the thing was empty-handed again, the thug reached out for a metal pipe leaning against a fence. The leader noticed the movement out of the corner of his eye and brandished his knife again.

Cold sweat dotted their foreheads. Only that unpleasant sensation kept their minds anchored to the reality before them.

"What the hell was that…a threat?" the leader growled, eyeing the bent club. A drop of sweat trickled down into his mouth, and he swallowed it. The thug barely noticed, gripping his pipe and panting heavily. His breathing grew steadily worse, until he realized that his legs, back, and chin were all trembling. The ostentatious club-bending performance had admirably served its menacing purpose.

The shadow started to walk closer, as though to confirm the effect of its show.

"Hand to hand, eh? At least you've got guts," the leader boldly declared. Unlike the thug, he'd made up his mind to fight. Eyes flashing, he approached the shadow, knife in hand.

It was three yards away. Two more steps, and he would be close enough to stab.

Gassan's a man who can use a knife when the time calls for it, the thug knew. He followed his leader, ready with his metal pipe.

The leader would take one more step, his hostility shifting to bloodlust, then with ultimate malevolence, he would stab the opponent. Only the knowledge that his boss was the kind of man to step across that line gave the thug the courage and security to follow behind him. There was no feeling of taboo about murder at this point, and the shadow itself was so unreal that the recognition of killing another human being didn't even apply here.

Sensing impending victory within his companion's aggression, the thug clenched his metal pipe harder. But the next moment, their hope for triumph was completely demolished.

The shadow seemed to reach around its back, and in the next moment, a part of its black form *swelled up*.

It was like stygian smoke erupting from the shadow, writhing with a will of its own. Black masses squirmed like black snakes out of the black shadow's black gloves.

The trail traced a vivid, eerie path through the air, like an inky brush dipped into a bucket of water. Eventually, the movement consolidated, building a form—a shape with meaning.

The two wide-eyed men finally saw, bathed in the light from the streetlamps and parking garage, that their foe was not human. They couldn't help but see.

In the instant when the black blob broke free from the shadow's body, something like charcoal soot escaped its form. It was as though the riding suit was melting away into the air, making everything aside from the helmet indistinct and hazy under the light.

Their brains were in a greater panic, now that they were fully isolated from the reality they'd known their entire lives. But with escape impossible, their bodies could only faithfully carry out the last orders they'd received. His expression locked in a nightmare rictus, the knife-bearing leader pulled back his weapon, pointing it at the shadow before him. After a moment of hesitation, he thrust the knife forward at the shadow's midriff, but...

The arm holding the knife shook with a dull shock before the blade reached the shadow. He did not drop it, but the impact rocked his stance enough to put him off-balance.

"?!"

The sharp, black form that hit the point of the knife began to take shape in the darkness.

It was dark, so dark. Darker than the darkest black. It absorbed the light around it, writhing and squirming like a living thing. Its nebulous, roiling form was terrifyingly hideous and primal, out of place in the modern streets of Japan.

But as soon as the shadow in its riding suit grabbed the thing, it began to blend into the scenery with an eerie awfulness.

The object in the shadow's hands was a dark, sunken hole in the midst of the night, an unmistakable symbol of death to anyone who saw it.

It was an enormous, double-sided scythe, nearly as long as the shadow was tall.

♂♀

—KANRA HAS ENTERED THE CHAT—
《I got disconnected. I dunno, my connection's been crap all day, so I'm just gonna go to bed.》
[Night.]
【What about the rest of the story? And who's Dotachin...?】
《I'll tell you later. Heh, oh, but one last thing.》

♂♀

The thug was truly trapped now.

There was no escape from the interior of the parking garage.

He didn't know what happened to the leader. He was not a bold enough man to stand around sussing out the details in a situation like that after what he'd just witnessed. On the other hand, he didn't see that giant scythe anymore. It occurred to him that it might've been nothing more than an illusion, but the answer was irrelevant to his circumstances at the moment, and he pushed the thought from his mind.

A powerful kick caught him on the neck. It sounded like something snapped, but there didn't appear to be anything wrong with the bone. Instead, the pain of a terrible stiff shoulder, concentrated into one acute spot, throbbed at the base of his neck.

But at this point, that detail mattered very little to the thug.

"Um, um, hang on, please, ple...please...p-p-puh-please, just hang on a second." The polite, pathetic stammering of one who is already beaten.

He knew what was happening to him. His senses were still unnerved and uneven, as though trapped in a dream, but the base, instinctual fear kept his mind locked into place and aware.

What he didn't understand was the reason. What *was* this shadow? What had he done to deserve this experience?

The most likely answer had to do with the job. Danger was an occupational fact of life, and enemies were a natural result. But those enemies were usually the police or mobsters or perhaps the targets of the job: illegal immigrants and runaway kids.

He knew the risks, and he conducted his job with the proper

attention to potential danger. But the shadow in the riding suit was completely outside the realm of expectations, and he had no idea how to react. He'd quickly lost the best and safest option—retreat—and was now trapped on all sides.

The only options he could think of were going down in flames or surrendering, but neither was a real choice as long as he could not grasp the enemy's intentions. Desperate for any means of survival, the thug wheedled and begged in his most pitiful whine. Perhaps using his voice was the only way to avoid being overtaken by fear entirely.

"P-please...spare me, you got the wrong guy, I didn't do nothin', forgive me, I'm sorry, I'm sorry!"

He bowed and scraped, covered in goose bumps, as though faced by a yakuza with his gun drawn. In contrast, the shadow simply stood silently as the thug shattered the illusion of his menacing appearance. It seemed to be searching for something—then abruptly turned its back on the thug and walked toward a van in the middle of the garage.

It was the kind of vehicle that often drove past Ikebukuro Station in the dead of night, rear windows tinted black, contents completely inscrutable to the outside.

The shadow walked straight for the van with unmistakable purpose, apparently seeing right through the black mirror.

Huh? ——Wha?! Oh, shit!

It was their "work" van. He still didn't know what the shadow wanted, but this made it clear the thing was after them. There were plenty of other vehicles in the garage, but it was heading straight for their car.

Wait! No, not that! Anything but that!

The thug's brain froze cold at the shadow's unpredictable actions. He'd been filled with a kind of primal fear at the presence of the shadow, but there was an entirely different kind of fear welling up in him now.

Aaaah, aaah, aaah! Wait, wait, waitwaitwait! You can't look in that van—we'll be done for! Shit, man, what do I do? What do I do? Shitshitshitshitshit—what is that? What is that thing?!

Two opposing fears wrestled for space in his conscious mind—the terror of the unreal sight and a much more grounded, realistic kind of fear.

If someone sees into that car, forget the police. I'll get buried!

His legs trembled even harder at the thought of his murdered corpse being disposed of in the forests at the foot of Mount Fuji.

There's gotta be something. Something I can use to murder that Kamen Rider freak...

The thug desperately searched for a way out of his situation now that he had ironically conquered his momentary fear of the shadow. What caught his eye was what he'd driven to the garage to report for work—his convertible.

Ten yards away from the van, the shadow stopped in silence.

From behind it came the faint sound of a car door opening and closing. As it turned around to see, the garage echoed with the blast of an engine revving.

"..."

At the end of its turn, the shadow caught sight of a bright red convertible speeding toward it. The car accelerated with surprising speed, and the shadow had no time to dart behind a pillar for safety.

After a moment of hesitation, it decided to run in the opposite direction of the approaching car. It was hoping to draw the car along and leap to the side at the last moment, but the terrified thug was using every ounce of his concentration and did not fall for it. The instant the shadow's foot turned to push it sideways, he yanked the wheel.

The sound of collision.

The shadow flew hideously through the air.

And crashed in a heap atop the concrete.

"Yeaaaaah! In your face! Ha-ha-haaa! In your ugly face, dammit!" the thug crowed, savoring the sensation of the shock that shuddered through the vehicle. He quickly braked and leaped out of the driver's seat before the car had even come to a stop, then raced for his victim, metal pipe in hand, when—

"?!"

He noticed a black blob rolling on the ground, much closer than the prone figure of the shadow.

There was no mistaking that distinct design—it was the full-faced helmet the shadow had been wearing just moments ago. But what shocked him was not the helmet...but the body of the shadow upon which it had been resting.

"The…the head…"

There was nothing atop the body where the shadow's head should be.

Did it come off in the crash?! No way can't be murder I didn't self-defense but no why hang on wait hang on

It was the latest shock in a long series. His brain was at a critical mass of confusion.

And because of that, he failed to notice that the body, now headless, had not shed a single drop of blood.

♂♀

《The guy riding the black motorcycle—has no head.》

♂♀

The thug hesitantly approached the headless body…

When without warning, the shadow leaped to its feet, still without a head.

♂♀

《He can totally move around without it.》
《Well, good night!》
—KANRA HAS LEFT THE CHAT—

♂♀

"Aaaahhh!!"

This sudden horrifying sight did not inflict fear on the thug as much as simple shock.

A trick?　　　　　　A suit?　　　　　　　A robot?
A costume party?　　A hologram?
A dream?　　An illusion?　　A hallucination?　　A fake?

Various words floated through his mind, popping like bubbles before his brain could grasp them.

The true shock was that it had been hit by a car yet was standing without any sign of harm whatsoever—but there was not enough conscious wit left in the thug's mind to dedicate to this fact.

As it had before, the black mist began to seep out of the shadow's back, taking shape as that gigantic scythe.

His shock shifting once again into fear, the thug began to let out a scream of terror and desperation. At the very moment his throat let the first bit of breath through, it was split by a sudden, sharp shock.

Every shred of his senses went black.

♂♀

<Private Mode> 【Um, Setton. I wanted to check something with you.】
<Private Mode> [Sure thing.]
<Private Mode> [What is it? Something you don't want others to see?]
<Private Mode> 【Is it just me, or is Kanra a little…corny?】
<Private Mode> [I'd say more than just a little.]
<Private Mode> 【You said it, not me (lol). But he was the one who invited me to this chat room, so…】
<Private Mode> [Same with me. He does get carried away, but that's part of his charm.]
<Private Mode> 【Plus, he seems to know many things we don't.】
<Private Mode> [I don't know how much of it is true, though. Oh, but I can say one thing.]

<Private Mode> [About that Black Rider who prowls around the town.]
<Private Mode> [You're probably better off not getting involved.]
<Private Mode> [Well, g'night.]

—SETTON HAS LEFT THE CHAT—

<Private Mode> 【Huh?】
<Private Mode> 【Whoa, Setton left. Well, good night.】
<Private Mode> 【Whatever.】

—TAROU TANAKA HAS LEFT THE CHAT—

♂♀

The headless rider quietly picked up the helmet and stuck it atop its dark neck. A faint shadow bled out of the collar of the suit, then melded into the bottom of the helmet, fusing it together.

Eventually, as though nothing had ever happened, the headless rider turned and silently strode toward the van.

Back at the entrance to the parking garage, having completed its business, the headless rider silently left the scene. Several men were lying in the street, but there was no sign that anyone else had passed by. If they had, they'd pretended not to see.

The pitch-black motorcycle waiting in the shadows sprang to life, welcoming its master home. The engine, which had worked soundlessly as it rode the streets, now roared without a key in the ignition.

The headless rider stroked the tank of the engine, like petting a beloved steed. The engine purred and hushed, satisfied, and the rider swung into the seat.

And the black mass, without so much as a headlight, carried its headless master away.

Beneath a starless sky.

Soundlessly melting into the darkness…

Headless Rider, Objective

Chapter 2

Center gate, Tobu Tojo Line, Ikebukuro Station, Toshima Ward, Tokyo

"I want to go home," the boy mumbled.

The statement was far too simple to encapsulate the myriad conflicting emotions he felt, but there was no other way to express his overall sentiment that directly.

Stretching out before his eyes were people. People, people, people. And more people. Basically people. His vision was overflowing with people as far as he could see. It was just past six in the evening, the time when many people started commuting home from work and school. It wasn't quite at peak levels yet, but the crowds were easily dense enough to be considered swarms.

He was so overwhelmed by the presence of people crammed into that vast underground space that the boy momentarily lost sight of his purpose for being there.

A salaryman bumped him with a shoulder. He started to apologize on instinct, but the man was gone, barely even conscious of what had happened. The boy bowed his head and mumbled an apology to no one and made his way over to one of the pillars a distance away from the gate.

The boy, Mikado Ryuugamine, felt a curious fluttering deep in his gut and decided that it came from anxiety. Despite his imposing name, there was weak-willed worry plain as day on his face.

It was his first-ever trip to Ikebukuro on the invitation of an old friend. To be more precise, it was his first trip to Tokyo at all—not just Ikebukuro—in his sixteen years of life.

He'd never been outside of the town where he grew up, and he'd stayed home for his class field trips in both elementary and middle school. He knew it was no way to go through life—and then he got accepted at a private high school in the Toshima Ward of Tokyo. It was a brand-new school built just a few years ago and was only a bit above average in school rankings, but it boasted one of the nicest campuses in the city. He had the option of going to school locally, of course, but it was his dream to live in the big city and an invitation from a childhood friend who moved away years ago that convinced him to make the leap.

This friend might have transferred away during elementary school, but Mikado had the Internet already at that age, and they chatted online nearly every day once in middle school. They hadn't seen each other in person during that time, but they weren't distant in any real sense.

Mikado's parents weren't used to the Internet, and the invitation of someone their son hadn't seen since elementary school was not a satisfactory reason to send him off to Tokyo. They didn't mention this, but they probably would have preferred to send him to a cheaper local public school. They argued, but Mikado convinced them by saying he'd raise his living funds outside of tuition by working jobs, and at last he was allowed to start a new chapter of his life in a new place.

"I think I've made a terrible mistake…"

He was feeling overwhelmed by the sheer number of people that would never bother to acknowledge his existence. He knew this was an illusion he himself was creating, but it was hard not to wonder if he would ever get used to this sensation.

After about the fifth sigh, he heard a familiar voice.

"Yo, Mikado!"

"?!"

He glanced up with a start to see a young man with his hair dyed brown. There was still a youthful softness to his face, which clashed somewhat with his hair and pierced ears.

Mikado was afraid he'd already been singled out for a shakedown or some kind of scam, then belatedly realized the person had called him by name. He glanced closer at the stranger and began to recognize the features of an old friend.

"Wait, um...Kida?"

"You have to ask? Okay, multiple choice: three answers. Am I, one, Masaomi Kida, two, Masaomi Kida, or, three, Masaomi Kida?"

For the first time since reaching Ikebukuro, Mikado smiled.

"Wow, Kida! Is that really you?"

"Thanks, just ignore the joke I spent three years crafting... Anyway, good to see you, man!"

"We were talking in chat just yesterday. Sorry, you look so different, I couldn't be sure it was you. I wasn't expecting your hair to be dyed! Also, that joke sucks."

Though they talked nearly every day online, there was no way for him to know how his friend's face had changed over the years. His voice was lower now, so it was little wonder he failed to recognize it at first.

Masaomi Kida smiled shyly and objected, "Well, it's been four years. And it's not that I've changed too much; you haven't changed *enough*. You look exactly the same as you did in elementary school...and don't slam my jokes." He smacked the top of Mikado's considerably more-youthful head a few times.

"Ack, knock it off. As if you've ever been shy about telling bad jokes in chat..."

Mikado swatted away his hand but wasn't really upset. First in school and later in the chat room, Masaomi had always been the one pulling Mikado along, and Mikado had never had a problem with that arrangement.

With their greeting out of the way, Masaomi started off through the crowd.

"Shall we take this outside, then? Go west, young man! Psych—we're heading for the Seibu exit, not the west exit. The trickster guide strikes again."

"Oh, I see. So what's the difference between the west exit and the Seibu exit?"

"...That joke fell flat."

Just from his short stroll with Masaomi, Mikado's fear of the crowd was already easing. Simply walking with another person who knew the town, an old familiar friend, made the sights of the big city vastly different in Mikado's eyes.

"See, outside of Ikebukuro Station, the Tobu (East Tokyo) Department Store is at the west exit, and the Seibu (West Tokyo) Department Store is at the east exit... Ugh, is there anything sadder than having to explain a failed joke? What does that make me?"

"Probably an idiot."

"...You've got a really sharp tongue, man," Masaomi grunted, grimacing as though he'd just chewed on a caterpillar. He sighed in resignation and muttered, "Whatever. Out of respect for myself, I will overlook that one. So, anything you wanna see in particular?"

"Well, like I mentioned in chat, I'd like to see Sunshine..."

"Right now? I mean...I'm fine with that, but you'll have a better time with a girlfriend."

Sunshine 60 was famous for once being the tallest building in Japan. Even after that record was broken by Tokyo City Hall and Landmark Tower, it was a bustling leisure destination, packed with students and families on the weekends thanks to its aquarium and the Namja Town amusement park.

He knew it was a lame answer, but Mikado couldn't think of any other place to go. Well, there was one place, something he recognized from a famous television show.

"Hey, what about Ikebukuro West Gate Park...?"

"Oh, I watched that show, too. Got the novels, the manga, everything."

"I'm not talking about the show, I mean the actual West Gate Park."

Masaomi looked stunned for a moment, then laughed in understanding.

"Oh, just call it Nishiguchi Koen in Japanese like normal."

"Huh? But...I thought all the Ikebukuroites called it by the English name."

"What's an Ikebukuroite? So what's up, you wanna go there?" Masaomi asked, stopping in his tracks. Mikado shook his head.

"N-no, let's not! It's almost nighttime! The color gangs will kill us!"

"Easy, buddy, don't act like it's some life-and-death matter. It's only six o'clock, for crying out loud! I see you're still a total coward."

Masaomi smiled exasperatedly and escorted Mikado through the crowd. It wasn't as dense here as it was outside of the ticket barrier, but it was still difficult for Mikado to maneuver without hitting anyone.

"There aren't as many color gangs anymore. There used to be a lot more of them you'd see around last year, but there was a big war with Saitama, and a few dozen of 'em got locked up. After that, anytime you got a few people wearing the same color together, the cops would rush 'em real quick. Plus, even at night, there's nothing crazy going on until at least after all the office workers and salarymen head home. The only exception is the big groups, like the *bosozoku* motorcycle gangs. Sometimes you see articles or news pieces on how they got into a big battle with the cops. Not here, but over in Kabukicho."

"*Bosozoku!*"

"But they're not gonna be hanging around the station at this hour is what I'm saying."

Mikado heaved a sigh of relief. "So is Ikebukuro safe these days?"

"I really only know half of what goes on, so this is partly guesswork. There are lots of color gangs and bikers around still, and there's plenty of dangerous stuff aside from them. Plus, even when it comes to ordinary people, there are some you can *never mess with*. Then again, you're not the type to go mad dogging people and picking fights. Just watch out for the pimps and shady businessmen and stay away from the thugs and *bosozoku*, and you'll be fine."

"I see."

Mikado couldn't help but wonder about the people "you can never mess with," but he didn't question Masaomi any further.

They headed down a narrower tunnel and onto the escalator leading up to the surface. Mikado glanced around and noticed enormous posters covering the entire wall. They featured various things—jewelers, upcoming movies, even a manga-style illustration of a girl.

When they reached the top of the escalator and exited onto the street, the air was still packed tight with people, and only the backdrop had changed.

Amid the unchanging sea of humanity, people in Windbreakers handed out tissue packets with business advertisements on the outside. Some handed them only to women, while others were less discriminate in their targets. Some of those who distributed only to men were very clearly singling out those worthy of their benefaction—Mikado was solidly ignored.

The crowds themselves were made up of a variety of people, from salarymen to the young and underemployed, teenage girls, even foreigners. But the crowd was not perfectly mixed; each type seemed to cluster with others of its ilk, forming distinct territories. Occasionally a person from one territory would venture forth and call out to a person of a different type. Even these sights were pushed along in the sheer wave of moving humanity.

This was a familiar phenomenon to Masaomi, but everything about it was exciting and new to Mikado. There had never been a sea of humanity like this back home, even at the largest shopping mall. He was witnessing a world he'd only ever seen on the Internet or in comic books.

When he related this to Masaomi, his friend laughed and said, "Next time I should take you to Shinjuku or Shibuya. Harajuku would be pretty good, too, if you want a real culture shock. There's also Akiba... but if you just want to see crowds, how about we hit up a racing track?"

"I'll pass," Mikado said politely. They'd exited onto one of the main roads. Cars raced busily down the multilane street, and there was a much larger road blocking the sky above them.

"That up there is the Metropolitan Expressway. Oh yeah, and the street we just took here is called Sixtieth Floor Street. There's also a Sunshine Street, but be careful not to get confused, because the Cinema Sunshine is actually on Sixtieth Floor Street. Dang, I should have shown you around that area since we just passed it."

"It's okay, we can do that another time," Mikado said. He was so distracted by the incredible crowds that he was failing to take in the sights of the city. At this rate, he'd never be able to get to Sunshine on his own from the station.

While they waited for the light to change, Masaomi looked back at the way they'd come and muttered, "I didn't see Simon or Shizuo today. I bet Yumasaki and Karisawa are at the arcade, though."

"Who?" Mikado asked automatically, though he knew Masaomi was just talking to himself.

"Uhh, Yumasaki and Karisawa are just people I know. Simon and Shizuo are two of those guys I was telling you about earlier—the ones you don't mess with. But as long as you lead a normal life, you don't

need to speak to Shizuo Heiwajima, and if you see him, your best bet is to run away."

Based on this statement, Mikado decided that Masaomi did not think highly of this Shizuo. Masaomi didn't offer anything else on the subject, so Mikado did not prod him further; instead, he asked about something else that was bothering him.

"These people you're not supposed to make enemies with—it sounds like something out of a comic book. Who else is there?"

It was an innocent question from a young man who looked like a boy, but Masaomi thought hard, looking up at the sky for answers. Finally, he declared his answer.

"First of all, there's me!"

"...Square root of three points."

"Square root?! What do you mean, square root?! If you're gonna blast me, at least go for an easy-to-understand joke like minus-twenty points! Are you saying my jokes are too hard to understand for kids who don't know how square roots work?! The instant I warn you, you make an enemy out of me! Since when were you such a dunce? Is it our education system? Has the system changed you, man?!"

"An unexpected downfall," Mikado replied without batting an eye to cut off Masaomi's spiel. He must have realized how obnoxious his monologue was getting as he continued in a serious tone this time.

"Hmm...there are a few. Obviously, you want to stay away from the yakuza and gangsters...but just in terms of people you might realistically come into contact with, there's the two I just mentioned and a guy named Izaya Orihara. He's bad news—you don't ever want to mess with him. He's from Shinjuku, though, so you'll probably never see him."

"Izaya Orihara...what a weird name."

"Coming from you?" Masaomi laughed.

He couldn't deny that one. Mikado Ryuugamine was an extremely overwrought name meaning "Emperor of the Peak of Dragons." In the past the family name had been a prestigious one, but his parents were plain old office workers. He didn't know much about the family finances, but if they were sitting on some sizable inheritance, they probably wouldn't have raised a fuss about his private school plans.

His given name was the part meaning "emperor" and was supposed to speak of a grand future, but the other kids in elementary school just made fun of him. People got used to it, though, and it never developed into full-blown bullying.

But unlike his school back home, where each grade only had one class with the same people in it, he was about to join a group of complete strangers in a totally new location. Would they see him as a man worthy of his name?

Probably not, Mikado thought.

Masaomi sensed his apprehension and tried to cheer him up.

"Hey, don't worry about it. It's a little fancy, but it's not a bad name. As long as you act like you own the place, no one can complain that your name doesn't suit you."

"...Yeah. Thanks," Mikado replied. The light turned green.

"Oh, speaking of guys you shouldn't mess with...you should steer clear of the Dollars."

"...Dollars."

"Yep. Not the Wanderers, the Dollars."

"Umm...whatever you say. So what kind of gang are they?" Mikado pressed, now driving the conversation rather than listening passively.

"I don't really know much about 'em. All I know is there's a lot of them, they've all got a screw loose, and they're supposed to be a gang. I don't know what color they rep, though. Then again, like I said, they're cracking down on the color gangs, so they might have broken up already for all I know."

"Oh, I see..."

An awkward silence settled between them. They walked across the intersection toward a sharply angled building across the street. There was a stylish automobile displayed inside the ground floor, which melded pleasingly with the striking design of the building itself.

Mikado was gazing at the building and its car, lost in thought, when he heard a strange voice.

The moment he heard it, Mikado thought it was like an animal roaring. But upon more careful consideration, it came from the middle of the street, far down the road. The next time it sounded, Mikado identified it as an engine. It still sounded like the growl of an animal, but given that it was coming from the street, it had to be the exhaust pipe of a car or motorcycle.

Mikado stopped in his tracks to watch the disturbance, but Masaomi simply watched calmly.

"You're lucky, Mikado."

"Huh?"

"You get an up-close-and-personal look at an urban legend on your very first day in the big city." Masaomi's face was expressionless, but there was a glint of hope and excitement in his eyes.

Speaking of which...

Mikado recalled other times that Masaomi's eyes had reflected that light. When he spotted a plane flying over the school in the middle of class. When he found a tanuki wandering onto the school grounds. Little occasions when the out of ordinary intruded upon the typical day.

He was unsure of how to get Masaomi's attention, when—

The *being* appeared before them.

A shadow in the shape of a person riding a pitch-black bike without a headlight.

It wove through the traffic—and passed by the boys without a sound.

"?!"

After several seconds, the engine roared again. But the next moment, it was once again silent, the only sound the faint screeching of tires on asphalt. It was so quiet that the engine had to be off entirely, but the motorcycle kept running without losing speed—it almost seemed to be accelerating, in fact.

It was a completely unreal thing, as though the area where its sound should have occurred had been cleanly removed from normal reality. Half the people walking along the street stopped, watching the shadow with suspicion.

That's when Mikado noticed that his entire body was trembling slightly.

It was not fear, but some other kind of emotion that had gripped his body.

I saw something incredible.

The moment they passed each other, Mikado gazed into the depths of the helmet. He couldn't actually see what was behind the visor, but he also didn't feel anything like a gaze emanating from the dead, still helmet.

Almost as though there was nothing inside of it to begin with.

♂♀

Chat room (late night)

—TAROU TANAKA HAS ENTERED THE CHAT—
【Good evening.】
[Evening.]
【Aha, Setton. I saw it today!】
【That Black Rider thing!】
[? Are you in Ikebukuro, Tarou Tanaka?]
【Yes. As a matter of fact, I just moved to Ikebukuro today. I'm logging in from a friend's house right now, but tomorrow I'll be living in an apartment next to the station. I've already signed up with an Internet provider, so I should be connected to the Net in no time.】
[Well, congrats. Living on your own?]
【Yes.】
[Ah, I see. So did you see the Black Rider around seven in the evening?]
【Oh, you know already? I saw it right outside Sunshine.】
[Yep. I was there.]
【?!】
【Really? Wow, we might have passed right by each other and never realized it!】
[Possibly.]
【Wow! Crazy! I should have mentioned this earlier, then!】
[At any rate, welcome to Ikebukuro. If there's anything you want to know, don't hesitate to ask.]
【Thank you very much!】
【Actually, in that case...】
[Yes?]
【Do you know someone named Izaya Orihara?】
【I was talking to my friend, and he said I should stay away from that guy.】
【Is he scary? Oh, what am I saying, you probably don't know him. Sorry.】
[...]

[Tarou Tanaka, is your friend one of...those people?]

【No, he's a normal guy.】

[Oh, I see. Sorry. You really shouldn't mess with Izaya Orihara. He's seriously bad news.]

《Oh! Good evening, Tanaka!》

【?! Kanra, have you been here all along?】

《I was just on the phone. Oh, I read the backlog, are you here in Tokyo? Congratulations! We should have an IRL welcoming party soon.》

【Oh, no need to go to all that trouble. I would like to hang out in person, though.】

《Yeah, I know.》

《Oh, speaking of meeting in person, you know those suicide groups?》

[Ahh.]

[Those were big last year. They'd meet on the Net and commit suicide together.]

【Eugh, creepy.】

【But I haven't seen anything about it in the news lately.】

[Either they're not going through with it anymore, or it's such old hat that the media doesn't even bother to report on it.]

《Or else it's happening all the time, and nobody's noticed yet!》

【Huh?】

《Like they just haven't found the bodies.》

【Gahh!】

[That's ghoulish.]

《But there really have been a lot of disappearances lately.》

【? Is that in the news?】

《I hear a lot about illegal immigrants and runaway children from the country vanishing, mostly from the Ikebukuro to Shibuya area. Some people say the Dollars are catching them and gobbling them up. Hee-hee!》

【So these Dollars really are famous around town.】

《The Dollars are crazy! Apparently they just had a run-in with the Chinese mafia, and when a yakuza got stabbed recently, it was supposedly the work of one of the Dollars' low-level guys!》

[Where are you getting this information, Kanra?]

《I know someone who knows this stuff. That's where I get my info.》

【Argh, I wanna know more, but I have to get up early tomorrow, so that's all for now.】

《Ah, good night, then!》
[Good night, Tarou Tanaka.]
[I have some business of my own, so I'm out as well.]
【Sorry to leave... Oh yeah, and tell me about this Dotachin person next time.】
【So long!】
《Well, I guess that's it for today. No one else is going to show up.》
《Good night. ☆》

—TAROU TANAKA HAS LEFT THE CHAT—
—SETTON HAS LEFT THE CHAT—
—KANRA HAS LEFT THE CHAT—

Headless Rider,
Subjective

Chapter 3

National Route 254 (Kawagoe Highway)

This really sucks.

The owner of the black bike—the headless rider—was in a foul mood as it rode the highway in the middle of the night.

It was supposed to be a simple job. And what was my reward for showing a bit of mercy? I got hit by a car. Should have shut him up from the start.

The headless rider slowed its speed, reflecting on the job it had been doing.

Without signal lights, it had to hand signal a left turn down a narrow side alley. It stopped before the garage of an apartment building, got off the motorcycle, and stroked its handlebars.

The engine gave a faint purr, and the vehicle *drove itself* into the garage.

Satisfied, the headless rider walked up to the entrance of the building.

"Hey, welcome home."

A young man in a lab coat greeted the rider inside an apartment on the top floor. He was a pleasant fellow in his midtwenties who matched the crisp coat, but there were no medical instruments to be seen inside the apartment. He looked quite out of place surrounded by the luxury furniture and electronics filling the room.

The shadow in the riding suit, looking equally out of place, stomped into the back room with apparent irritation.

"Uh-oh, someone's angry. You need a higher calcium intake," the man in the lab coat said, pulling the chair out from a computer desk in a corner of the room. He sat down and turned to the screen, and the sound of clicking keys came rattling from the back room.

Text appeared on the monitor in front of the man in the coat. The two computers were connected in a LAN configuration, arranged so that they could talk to one another.

"Am I supposed to eat eggshells?"

"Sure, why not? Then again, I don't know much about nutrition, so I don't know how much calcium is in eggshells or how efficient a means of intake that is. There's also the question of how necessary calcium really is when I don't know even know where your brain is. How do you eat, anyway?"

The man in the coat did not type at his keyboard, but spoke out loud to the headless rider in the back. The rider rattled the keyboard with another message, not bothered by this one-sided conversation.

"Shut up."

This was apparently how the man in the lab coat and the headless rider communicated, a means of conversation that worked for both.

"All right, I'll shut up. On another topic, staring at a computer monitor all day wears out a human being's eyes. What about you?"

"How should I know?"

"Say, Celty. If you don't have any eyeballs, how do you perceive the world around you? I keep asking, but you never tell me."

"I can't explain something I don't understand myself."

The shadow—named Celty—had no head. Therefore, it had no organs to sense sight or sound. But in Celty's world, there *was* sight and sound and even smell. Celty could read the letters on the screen and make out even subtle color differences in crisp detail. The one difference was that Celty could see a slightly wider range of things at a glance than a human could. But only slightly—if Celty could see all around at once, that nasty collision with the car would not have happened.

Celty's vision generally came from where the head would be, but it was also adjustable to come from any other part of the body. The only thing that wasn't possible was a disengaged bird's-eye view.

Even Celty did not know exactly how this body worked. And as Celty did not know how a human being saw the world, there was no good way to explain the difference between them.

Noticing Celty's silence on the monitor, Shinra offered his own explanation.

"Here's my hypothesis: It's that strange, sci-fi-worthy, shadowlike substance that issues endlessly from your body. I've never observed this for myself, but I think you emit that into the environment around you, then reabsorb it when it reflects back toward your body, carrying information with it. Your shadow brings back light, sound, and smell. Like a radar. Naturally, things that are farther away will return less certain information. Perhaps that shadow you wear about you acts as a sensory organ, acquiring light, vibrations, even scent particles."

"I have no interest in your nonsense. I can see and hear, and that's all I need," came the clipped, typed response.

The man in the lab coat shrugged theatrically.

"You've always been like this, Celty. I just want to know what the difference is between the world I feel and the world you feel... It's not an issue of your eyesight. It's an issue of your values. Not your human values..."

He paused for a breath, then continued callously, "...But the values of *a fairy manifested into physical form in this city—a dullahan.*"

Celty Sturluson was not a human being.

Celty was a type of fairy known as a dullahan that appeared to those close to death, signaling their impending demise. The dullahan carries its own severed head under its arm and rides on a two-wheeled carriage called a Coiste Bodhar, pulled by a headless horse. When it arrives at the home of the soon to be dead, anyone careless enough to open the door gets a basin of blood thrown upon them. Like the banshee, tales of this eerie messenger echoed throughout Europe for centuries.

This would not normally be known in Japan, but recognition of the dullahan exploded thanks to the influence of fantasy novels and video games. As harbingers of misfortune, dullahans were well suited to playing villains, and their image as ghastly knights of the dead made them popular among fans of games and adventure stories.

But Celty had come to Japan from Ireland, the ancestral home of the dullahans, unrelated to any of that development.

The details of Celty's birth, why a basin of blood was necessary, and why humans needed to be told of their deaths were all things lost to the murky, unremembered past. And in order to get them back... Celty was now on this island nation halfway around the world.

About twenty years ago, Celty awakened in the mountains and realized that many memories were missing.

These included details such as the reason for Celty's actions and any memory of the past beyond a certain point—all that Celty could remember was being a dullahan, the name Celty Sturluson, and how to use those powers. When the nearby headless horse came over for a pat on the back, Celty finally noticed that the horse wasn't the only one without a head.

The first shock was, *I'm not actually thinking with my head?!* Next, Celty was surprised to realize that the head, wherever it was, was giving off some kind of vaguely detectable aura.

After further reflection, a conclusion formed. Celty's consciousness was shared between body and head, and it was inside the head that those missing memories existed. Thus, Celty came to an immediate decision. The head that contained all the secrets, the reasons for existence, must be regained. For now, that *was* Celty's reason for existing. Perhaps the head had strayed from the body of its own will—but that would not be known until Celty found it, either way.

The only option was to sense the faint traces of that aura in search of the head—which led Celty to a boat that crossed the seas. It soon became clear that the boat was headed for Japan, which was exactly the right destination. Celty had successfully stowed away—the problem was the headless horse and two-wheeled carriage.

These two things—possessed dead horse and carriage—were like familiars to a dullahan and could be erased if so desired. But where would they go after that? The knowledge was probably contained in Celty's missing head. Given that drawback, it was difficult to go through with the act, even if Celty *did* know how to do it. The dullahan gave it some thought and proceeded to a scrapyard near the port.

That's where Celty found the perfect replacement, something that looked like the fusion of carriage and horse: a black vehicle with no headlight and two wheels.

Twenty years had passed since Celty arrived in Japan. No clues yet.

The aura that Celty sensed was something like a faint smell—it would point in a very general direction, but once within a reasonable range of the target, it was no longer any help at all.

I know it's somewhere here in Tokyo, Celty insisted and continued the search for the missing head.

Whether it took years or decades, Celty had no misgivings. The oldest surviving memories went back centuries. The ones still hidden in the head had to be even older.

Based on this knowledge, time was apparently relatively meaningless to a dullahan. The only factor that caused Celty to hasten was the uncertainty of what could be happening to the head.

Tonight, Celty would once again race through the dark streets of Tokyo.

While performing a side job as a courier.

"I presume you performed your duties with all due diligence?" asked Shinra Kishitani, the man in the lab coat, without a trace of irony at his alliteration. He was one of the few human beings who knew what Celty was and provided a variety of jobs to complete, offering a place to stay in return.

He was the son of a doctor who'd been on the ship Celty had snuck onto and had found the dullahan while they were at sea. His father had a simple request, delivered in writing.

"Let me dissect you just once, and you will have a place to live."

Shinra's father was an abnormal man. Faced with this unexplained, intelligent being, he did not cower in fear, but proposed a deal. Furthermore, he did not announce his findings to the scientific community, but kept them himself as a sheer sign of his own curiosity. Apparently Celty's native healing power was phenomenal—the incisions practically knitted themselves closed over the course of the dissection.

Celty did not have much memory of the operation.

The shock of the dissection was probably to blame for most of that. They'd used an anesthetic, but the human concoction did not work on Celty. The pain of the incision was vivid and sharp, but Celty's limbs had been tied down with heavy chains to prevent struggle. Apparently the dullahan had passed out in the middle of the dissection, as Celty did not remember anything after that.

"You do seem to have some sense of pain but much duller than a human's. A normal person would have been driven mad by that," Shinra's father announced after the operation. Without any memory of the incident, Celty didn't have the willpower to be angered by this anymore.

Based on the very quick recovery after being hit by the car tonight, it was certain that Celty's body was very tough indeed. The dullahan looked over at Shinra.

Shinra's father had seen to it that his son was present during the dissection. He put a glinting scalpel into the five-year-old's hand—and ordered him to split open the flesh of what looked very much like a human being.

Upon learning this, Celty suspected that being raised by such a father would do Shinra's personal development no favors—and he had turned out just as twisted as his predecessor.

At the age of twenty-four, Shinra styled himself as a traveling underground doctor, taking on patients that doctors aboveboard found inconvenient for various reasons—typically victims of gunshot wounds, as guns were illegal in Japan, or those who needed facial surgery they didn't want public. He had extraordinary skill and standing for a doctor his age (in fact, most doctors couldn't do what he did), but that was again all according to Shinra himself, and Celty couldn't tell if any of it was true. Normally, properly licensed doctors had to serve as assistants in several hundred operations before they were allowed to be surgeons, and as far as Celty could tell, Shinra had achieved easily that much experience illegally assisting his father's experiments. Like father, like son; by the time he graduated high school, Shinra had no qualms about what he did.

And now this man was asking Celty about the night's work progress with a straight face.

"It was absolutely infuriating," Celty commented to Shinra with a hint of sarcasm, then hunched over to start typing out the night's events in earnest.

Tonight's job had been a special one, and Shinra brought it up quite suddenly after night had already fallen.

There was a group of kids that hung out together in Ikebukuro, and one of them had been abducted. Normally this was the job of the police to handle, but time was of the essence, so the text came directly to them.

Abduction was the job of the lowest of the lowest of the low on the totem pole of any evil enterprise. They'd kidnap illegal immigrants or runaway kids, then hand them over to the next highest group in the hierarchy. The exact purpose of this scheme was unclear, but it was probably a business that required "human goods." Perhaps their superiors' superiors' superiors needed them for human experimentation, or perhaps the superiors' superiors wanted them for some kind of nefarious business scheme. Either that or the direct superiors simply hoped to sell them off somewhere else for a quick buck.

For whatever reason, their friend, who was staying in the country illegally, had been taken. The idea of this illegal immigrant friend didn't appeal very much, but without a face or identity, Celty had no other way to work for a living than doing these jobs.

In the end, the abductors were solidly beaten and the van was spotted. After ensuring the victims were safe, Celty sent a text to Shinra. Following that, Shinra presumably contacted the group of friends directly. Whatever happened to the unconscious kidnappers after that was a mystery.

Why not just tell the group where the people were and let them do their own dirty work? But Shinra wanted it to be done stealthily, so the job fell to Celty. Rather than let it turn into a big, messy fight between two groups of people, have one experienced professional slip in and do the job clinically and quietly.

And because of that, Celty had been run over by a car. The dullahan didn't end up killing anyone, but that shadow scythe had caused much pain.

Celty was *wreathed in shadow* at all times. Sometimes it took the form of armor, but through acts of willpower, it could be turned into that familiar riding suit or even simple weapons.

The idea of a shadow having mass was silly, but the shadow that wrapped Celty's body was quite light and could be used to perform all kinds of stunts worthy of an action movie. But because the shadow had nearly no weight of its own, Celty's strength was entirely responsible for the force of the blows. Still, the blade itself was perfectly sharp and tough—as far as Celty could remember, it had never chipped. It was like the sharpness and weight of an indestructible razor blade, with the size of a katana.

The shadow was no use as a bludgeon, but it held incredible force when shaped into a blade. But Celty chose not to cut the thugs with the scythe, knocking them out with a handle jab to the throat instead. Centuries ago, Celty could vaguely remember slicing up people back home who had shrieked about monsters when faced with the dullahan. But that was not an option in modern Japan.

In the past twenty years, Celty had learned Japanese and a kind of self-control to avoid killing foes. The best way to learn would have been an aikido, self-defense, or karate dojo, but none of those in the area would take a pupil who wore a helmet indoors.

As it happened, the scythe was not a convenient tool for a weapon. The menace it held in the hands of the Grim Reaper made it seem deadly, but in reality, swords and spears were much easier to use. But Celty continued to wield the shadow in the form of a giant scythe because, as Shinra put it, "You get your name out better that way."

Even worse, Celty was gradually growing to like the shape of the weapon. But no amount of visual menace helped when you got run over by a car. The pain had long faded, but the irritation at the carelessness that caused it bubbled and boiled on the inside.

There was no knowing how much damage would actually be fatal. Celty had never tested it and never planned to. With that in mind, the dullahan reported the evening's events to Shinra.

He merely grinned at the gruesome details of vehicular carnage.

"Well, you've earned a break for your good work. Speaking of which, one more thing."

"*Which is?*"

"The reason we figured out where our target was being held so quickly was because I asked Orihara."

Izaya Orihara. He was an information agent based out of Shinjuku, a man who sold various pieces of valuable information for great sums of cash. That apparently was not his main job, and no one knew what he got up to in private.

They'd taken on a number of jobs for him, and many of them left a bad aftertaste. Frankly, Celty did not think it a good idea to be involved with Izaya.

"Why him?"

"Well, we'd just gotten that call, so in exchange for the payment, I asked if he knew anything about the number of the car, and he came back with the location of that parking garage immediately."

Celty ground nonexistent teeth at that. It was strange that even without a head, the sensation of gritted teeth should still be so vivid. The dullahan was wondering where that feeling was actually coming from when Shinra leaned over and clapped his hands on Celty's shoulders. He'd walked into the back room during that idle contemplation.

"So, have you made up your mind yet?"

"About what?"

Shinra looked down at the screen to read the text, then smiled painfully.

"You know," he continued before the next message was even typed into the computer, "you are an elusive and fantastical being, Celty. But at this rate, you may not reach your goal for eons."

"What are you trying to say?"

"I'll make it clear and simple. *Give up.*"

The sound of typing stopped, and the room was enveloped in an eerie silence.

"Forget about looking for your head. Let's go somewhere together. Anywhere, really. If you want to go back home, I'll do anything I can to get you there. And I'll come with you—"

When Shinra stopped talking in fanciful vocabulary terms, it was a sign that he was sincerely engaging in the conversation.

"How many times must I tell you? I have no intention of giving up."

"Everywhere around the world, there are myths and folktales of the headless wandering in search of their heads. There must have been more like you in the past. They even made a movie about the story of Sleepy Hollow, which means there must have been someone like you back in the 1800s. Maybe that *was* you, and you've simply forgotten your memory of it," Shinra blabbered on.

Celty patiently typed out a response.

"Why would I want to kidnap a boring schoolteacher?"

"Wow, going straight back to the original novel..."

Celty continued touch-typing with no small amount of irritation, smacking his hand away.

"I don't dislike you, but living with you like this is enough for now."

Shinra stared down at the lonely text on the screen and murmured.

"In that case, you could at least stand to be a *bit more feminine.*"

A brief pause. The difference in warmth between them almost seemed to crack the air.

"Enough of this. I'm taking a shower."

Celty showered alone in the steamy bathroom. Her body was as perfect as any model's: shapely breasts and tight stomach. But because of that, it only made the lack of a head creepier.

She concentrated on the mirror as her soapy fingers caressed the silky skin. The sight of a naked, headless woman sudsing up was surreal, to say the least, but it did not bother her at all anymore.

Back in Ireland, she had never showered, but after coming to Japan, she steadily became accustomed to the practice. It had nothing to do with her body, and she never had to deal with sweat and grime, but in the sense of removing any buildup of dust, she couldn't imagine not having regular showers anymore.

Maybe this is proof that I've developed the same values as humans.

Celty constantly wondered if her dullahan values were indeed coming to resemble a human being's. She'd been constantly baffled after her initial arrival to Japan, but now she felt as though the Japanese mind-set had rubbed off on her.

Recently, she was viewing Shinra acutely as a member of the opposite sex more and more often. At first she was confused—but in time, she recognized that it must be the sensation of love. But Celty was not a girl trapped in the clutches of puberty, and this realization did not affect her daily life.

But she did notice the little things. It made her happy when they were watching TV and Shinra laughed at the same moments she did.

I have the same values as a human being. I have the same heart. And my heart can find common ground with a human's—I think.

At least, that was what she wanted to believe.

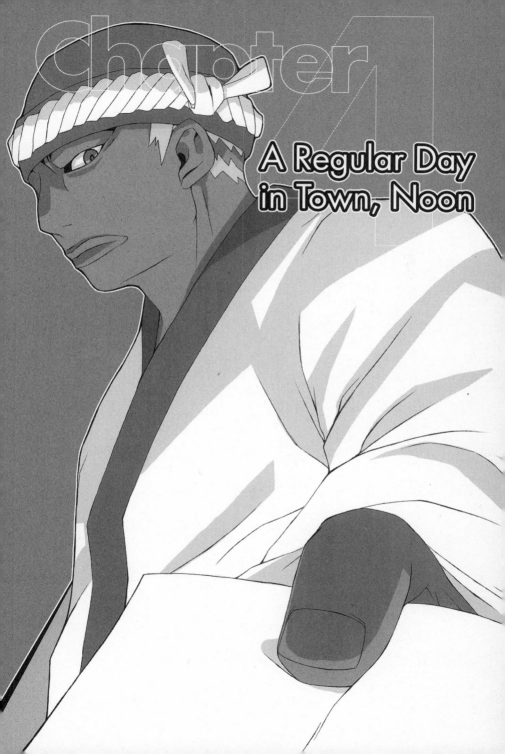

chapter 4

A Regular Day in Town, Noon

Raira Academy was a coed private high school in south Ikebukuro.

Despite its modest size, the campus maximized the utility of its limited space, and therefore, the students did not see it as particularly cramped. Its proximity to Ikebukuro Station made it increasingly popular with people from the suburbs of Tokyo, who could commute to school while still living at home. The school's ranking and prestige were on a gentle upward climb, so the timing of Mikado's arrival was actually quite fortunate.

The elevated location gave the campus an excellent view, but any feeling of superiority instantly evaporated upon the sight of the sixty-floor building looming overhead. On the other side of the school was the expanse of Zoshigaya Cemetery, a lonely place for being in the middle of a giant city.

The entrance ceremony was anticlimactically short, and Mikado and Masaomi split off to their own classes for a brief homeroom session.

"My name is Mikado Ryuugamine. It's nice to meet you."

Mikado was worried about being teased about his name, but there was no reaction to his introduction. Apparently the people of his generation were even less interested in others' names than Mikado expected. Despite this, he listened intently to his classmates' introductions, eager to learn as much as he could about them.

Some cracked easy jokes as they introduced themselves, and some said their names and sat down immediately. Some were already fast asleep, but most interesting of all to Mikado was a girl named Anri Sonohara. She was small for a high schooler, and her pale, pretty face was framed with glasses, but there was a distant air of foreboding about her—not intimidating to others, but one that suggested she did not usually reach out voluntarily.

"My name is Anri Sonohara."

Her voice seemed to vanish as soon as it hit the air, but Mikado caught its clear inflection perfectly fine. Anri stood out to Mikado among the class because she seemed to be the most removed from reality. All the other people were just plain high schoolers, without any obvious model students or bad boys.

The only other thing out of place was that one person in Mikado's class was absent. Her name was Mika Harima, but he soon reasoned away her absence by assuming it was the flu.

However, the instant her absence was announced, Anri Sonohara quickly looked over to the empty seat with concern plain on her face.

After that, homeroom ended uneventfully, and he met up with Masaomi, who was in the class next door.

Masaomi still had his daring earrings in, but he didn't particularly stick out from the crowd. In fact, Mikado seemed to be more noticeable, perhaps because the school allowed regular clothes. They were both wearing the school blazer as instructed for the ceremony, but otherwise they didn't even appear to be students at the same school.

"Well, we didn't get to hang out yesterday because of your moving in and getting Internet access and all. I'll show you somewhere today if you buy me a meal," Masaomi offered. Mikado had no reason to refuse. Clubs were forbidden from canvassing for new members until later, so they were able to leave campus without being harassed. The Sunshine 60 building loomed in the corner of their eyes as they headed for the shopping district.

Ikebukuro was a mysterious place to Mikado. Each major street seemed to have its own distinct culture; he felt a bewildering new alienation with each and every block.

"Anyplace you wanna go?"

"Uhm… Where's a bookstore?" Mikado asked in front of a fast-food place at the entrance to 60-Kai Street. Masaomi thought it over.

"Well, if you want books, our best bet around here is Junkudo… What are you looking for?"

"I guess I'd like some manga to read once I get back home…"

Masaomi started walking in silence.

"There's a place down that way that sells a ton of manga. Let's go there."

He made his way to an intersection with an arcade, then turned right. It had yet another totally different vibe than 60-Kai Street, and Mikado couldn't help feeling like he'd wandered into a different neighborhood again. At this point, it still took all of Mikado's concentration to get from his train stop to his apartment, and he felt that one wrong turn down an alleyway was a mistake from which he'd never recover to find his bearings.

"It looks like they sell lots of *doujinshi* here, too."

Doujinshi. As a resident of the Net, Mikado was not a total stranger to the fan-made manga zines, but he'd never bought one for himself. He remembered some of the girls from middle school squealing over them, but from what he knew based on the Internet, they were all sexually explicit and age restricted to buyers eighteen or older.

"A-are we even allowed inside? Won't they yell at us?"

"Huh?" Masaomi shot back, completely bewildered. Suddenly, a voice called out to them.

"Hey, it's Kida."

"Long time no see!"

"Aha, Karisawa and Yumasaki! Hi."

It was a boy and a girl. They both seemed extremely pale for people appearing outside in the middle of the day. The boy was spindly with a sharp gaze and he carried a heavy-looking backpack, but he didn't seem to be preparing for a camping trip, as far as Mikado could tell.

The girl asked Masaomi, "Who's this? A friend?"

"Oh, he's a longtime friend. We just started at the same school."

"So today was your first day of high school? Congrats."

Masaomi finally got around to introducing the two.

"The girl here is Karisawa, and the guy is Yumasaki."

"…Ah…umm…my name's Mikado Ryuugamine."

The guy named Yumasaki tilted his head when he heard the name. It was incredibly affected and made him look like a figurine. He ignored the confused Mikado and turned to Karisawa.

"Is that a pen name?"

"Why would a first-year high school student introduce himself with a pen name? Are you talking about the kind you use to submit letters to a radio show or magazine?"

"Um, actually, it's my real name," Mikado mumbled.

Their eyes widened.

"No way, it's real?!"

"That's awesome! That's so cool! You're like the protagonist of a manga or something!" Karisawa and Yumasaki raved.

"Geez... You're making me feel self-conscious."

"Why would *you* feel self-conscious, Kida?"

Left out of a conversation entirely about himself, Mikado was at a loss for what to do. Eventually Yumasaki noticed his awkward distance and briefly checked the time on his cell phone.

"Okay, okay, sorry to take up your time. You were heading somewhere, weren't you?"

"No, we weren't in any kind of rush," Mikado responded with a rapid shake of his head, feeling even more self-conscious now.

"No, it's okay, it's okay. Sorry for taking up your time, Kida."

"We're just off to hit up all the arcades. Are you on a shopping trip?"

"Yes, we're picking up some manga."

At this, Yumasaki reached a hand around his back and patted his backpack. "Hey, that's just what we were doing before this. All the latest Dengeki Bunko titles just came out, so I bought a ton of 'em. About thirty in total, I think."

He'd heard of the name Dengeki Bunko. That was a publishing label that specialized in light novels and translations of Hollywood movie novelizations. Mikado had even bought some books from Dengeki in middle school, but thirty was clearly overkill.

"Does Dengeki Bunko really put out that many books a month?"

Karisawa cackled and answered, "Don't be silly! We got two copies of each one for the both of us, plus about ten more to use tonight!"

"*Also,* I picked up *Moezan*, the quiz book of burning-hot math problems. With Jubby Shimamoto's autograph and everything," Yumasaki boasted. Mikado didn't understand a single word of what he said and looked to Masaomi for clarification.

"...Just ignore him—think of whatever he's saying as magic spells. These two are the kind of weirdos who assume that everyone else knows what they know," Masaomi whispered to Mikado. Yumasaki continued prattling on about even more obscure subjects, but Karisawa noticed the effect it was having on the other two and jabbed her partner's backpack with an elbow.

"Quit bragging to the norms. We'll just be on our way. Bye!"

Mikado watched the two shuffle off, then wondered under his breath, "Books to...use tonight...?"

He had no idea what they were going to "use" the books for, but they were already leaving and there was no point in calling them back to ask, so Mikado turned and followed Masaomi to the bookstore.

"Wow, that selection was incredible! I was amazed! That Toranoana place had more manga alone than any bookstore back home!"

"Yeah, there are plenty of places in Ikebukuro where you can find tons of manga, like Animate or Comic Plaza. And if you want anything non-manga, Junkudo's the place to go. It's a building about nine stories tall, all books."

They had finished their shopping at the bookstore and were walking down 60-Kai Street toward the Sunshine building.

"I didn't realize you knew people like them, Kida."

"You mean Karisawa and Yumasaki? What, are you saying you thought I'd only be friends with people with bleached-blond hair, piercings, and brains addled from huffing paint? Well, as it happens, those two are plenty weird on their own, but they're nice if you act cool around 'em."

"I...see."

Something about that struck Mikado as weird, but he decided to ignore it rather than press for more information.

"Basically, I poke my head into all kinds of places. Bookstores like that, where to find the cheapest vintage clothes, directions to hole-in-the-wall clubs and bars, even street-side accessory shops—I've got a handle on all these things."

"Seems like you know just about everything."

"If you can speak about any topic, you can tailor the conversation to mack on any type of girl."

"Such impure motives," Mikado groaned. Masaomi grinned and nodded confidently.

Today, Mikado was determined to take in as much of the scenery as possible, and he kept his eyes up as he traveled rather than tracing the ground.

Standing out first and foremost along the street were the huge video screens hanging on the Cinema Sunshine building and the many movie posters lining the adjacent walls. They looked like photos, but Mikado was stunned to realize on closer examination that they were all illustrations fashioned to look like realistic photographs.

He swiveled to see what other stores were around, then caught something more arresting than any building.

"Huh?"

It was just one of the many black solicitors that lined this street—but this one was different.

He was at least six feet tall and covered with thick, ropy muscle that made him look like a wrestler. Even more striking was the *itamae* sushi chef outfit he wore to entice customers to his business.

Mikado stared wide-eyed, when suddenly the large man noticed him.

"Nice see you again, bro."

"!?!?!"

Mikado had no idea how to respond. He'd never seen this man in his life, yet was being greeted in the form of a reunion. Just when he thought his smooth sailing in Tokyo was about to come to a crashing end, Masaomi rescued him.

"Hey, Simon! Long time no see! How's it hangin', man?"

The large man's attention switched from Mikado to his friend.

"Hey, Kida. Eat sushi? Sushi good. I make cheap deal. You like sushi?"

"Not today, Simon, I'm broke. I just started high school, so I can start working a part-time job. How about you give me free sushi now, and I pay you back then?"

"No can do. Then I sleep with fishes on Russian motherland."

"With fishes? On land?" Masaomi chuckled and left the conversation hanging.

Mikado hurried after him, turning back to Simon to see the large black man waving at them. Bewildered and unaware of how to react, Mikado bowed briefly in apology.

"You know that guy, too?"

"Oh, Simon? He's an Afro-Russian, and he helps draw customers for a sushi place run by Russians."

Afro-Russian?

"Sorry, which part of that was the joke?"

"No, I'm serious. His actual name is Semyon, but everyone just calls him the English version of that, Simon. I don't know the whole story, but apparently his parents emigrated there from America. Some other Russian folks he knew were starting up a sushi restaurant, so he works the street, getting the word out."

None of it sounded real, but there was only pure sincerity in Masaomi's eyes. It had to be true. Mikado was still wide-eyed in disbelief, so Masaomi added, "He's one of those guys you're not supposed to cross. Once I saw him pick up two guys who were brawling off the ground with one hand each, both of them his size. Word says he broke a telephone pole in half once, too."

Mikado shivered, envisioning that tanklike build again. After a few more moments of walking, he murmured, "This is amazing."

"Huh? What is?"

"That you can talk to so many different kinds of people, I mean..."

Mikado meant it as an honest compliment, but Masaomi just laughed it off as a joke. He cackled and yawned, shrugging it away.

"Oh no, you can't butter me up like that."

"I'm not."

In fact, Mikado had tremendous respect for Masaomi. If he'd been alone, he would have dried up and shriveled amid the sea of humanity that was Ikebukuro. The people who lived here were not all like Masaomi. Ever since grade school, he'd had a special charm that drew others to him, and he had the assurance to speak for himself in any situation.

How many times had he been blown away by both the neighborhood and Masaomi in just the few days since arriving? Mikado hoped that one day he could be like his friend.

One of the biggest reasons for Mikado's exodus to the big city was to escape the familiar sights of his world. This was not a tangible thought at the forefront of his mind, but deep within his heart, he was constantly searching for a "new self." Perhaps in this place, he'd find the "extraordinary" that existed in comic books and TV shows and experience it for himself.

Mikado didn't want to be a hero. He just wanted to feel a different kind of breeze through his hair. He didn't realize it himself, but amid that terrible anxiety deep in his gut on that first visit to Ikebukuro was a powerful elation and excitement that fought for control with his unease.

And right next to him was someone who had mastered the fresh breeze of his new home, harnessed that excitement for himself. Even at age sixteen, Masaomi had completely blended into this place and made himself a part of it.

Mikado realized that his friend represented everything that he wanted, and the warring anxiety and excitement lulled as he felt more in control of his surroundings—or at least, they should have.

But in the next moment, all of that was destroyed as a fresh new maelstrom of anxiety and excitement burst into life.

"Hey."

It was a very pleasant voice, crisp and clear and vibrant, as though being hailed by the pure blue sky itself.

And yet, the instant he heard that voice, Masaomi grimaced as though he'd been shot in the back with arrows. He slowly turned in the direction of the voice, an instant sweat congealing on his face.

Mikado turned the same way and saw a young man with an equally pleasant face. He looked soft and gentle, but with a bold, intrepid edge—a perfect materialization of some ideal of handsomeness. His eyes were warm and all-accepting but glinted with a hard scorn of anything that wasn't himself. His outfit, while possessing its own personality, did not show off any obvious features or characteristics. All in all, he was very difficult to grasp or classify.

Even his age was indistinct based on appearance alone. He had to be more than twenty at least, but there was no way to tell anything beyond that.

"Nice to see you again, Masaomi Kida."

Masaomi responded to the use of his full name with an expression Mikado had never seen before and swallowed.

"Ah… H…hi," he responded awkwardly.

Mikado's state of mind erupted into chaos. *I don't think I've ever seen Kida look like this…*

Fear and disgust mingled in Masaomi's eyes, but the muscles in his face were tense, trying to bottle up that emotion.

"Is that a Raira Academy uniform? So you got in. First day of school? Congrats."

His congratulations were brief and clipped, but not devoid of feeling. He only used the barest minimum of emotion necessary in his voice, however.

"Y-yes, thanks to you," Masaomi said, a common pleasantry.

"I didn't do a thing."

"It's strange to see you out in Ikebukuro…"

"I'm just meeting some friends. And who's that?"

The man looked at Mikado, and for an instant, their eyes met. Normally, Mikado would look away shyly, but this time he couldn't tear his eyes away. He felt as though if he broke that contact, his entire existence would be denied, negated. Mikado didn't know why he felt this way—the man's gaze simply held him in place with its breathtaking sharpness.

"Er, he's just a friend," Masaomi blurted. Normally he would have said Mikado's name, but he seemed to be intentionally avoiding that. The man did not seem perturbed by this omission in any way. He turned to Mikado.

"I'm Izaya Orihara. Nice to meet you."

Everything clicked into place for Mikado. The man not to get involved with. The man not to make an enemy out of. But the fellow standing before him didn't seem all that dangerous. Aside from his sharp gaze and handsome features, he seemed like any other young man. Even his plain, glossy black hair stood out amid all the bleached and dyed hair around him. He looked like the kind of sharp young man that would be teaching at a cram school out in the country somewhere.

He's more normal than I expected, Mikado thought, and decided to introduce himself.

"Sounds like an air conditioner," came Izaya's response, without mirth or surprise. He seemed to be referring to the Kirigamine appliance brand. Mikado opened his mouth, unsure of whether or not he should say something to continue the conversation, when Izaya raised a hand.

"Well, it's time for my meeting. Gotta go."

And with that, he left. Masaomi stretched and inhaled a deep breath, watching Izaya's retreating back.

"C'mon, let's go. Uh, where were we off to?"

"Is he really that scary?"

"Scary might not be the right word... See, I got into my share of trouble in middle school...and I ran into him once, and it really scared me. It's not like a yakuza thing—he's just *unstable*. He's unpredictable. His motives and beliefs change every five seconds. The fear he inspires isn't one of danger...it's more like he makes me sick. One of those creepy-crawly feelings that sneaks up on you. I'm never going to the *other side* again. If you ever wanna smoke ganja or whatever, don't look to me for help."

Ganja. Mikado shook his head abruptly. He'd never seen it in person, but he'd been on the Internet long enough to know exactly what that was.

"I'm just kidding, man. You're the kind of guy who won't drink or smoke until the legal age at twenty. Just stay away from him and Shizuo Heiwajima. That's rule number one."

Masaomi clearly didn't want to say another word about Izaya, so they kept walking in silence for a while. Mikado had never seen Masaomi like this before. More than Izaya, it was Masaomi's attitude that had piqued his curiosity.

Maybe there's no limit to the kind of extraordinary things I can experience here, Mikado thought. It was a stretch from what prompted the notion, but he could feel his excitement and expectation growing from within.

It had only been a few days since Mikado came to Ikebukuro. But already, the phrase *return home* had disappeared from his dictionary.

Those crowds of people, which had seemed so artificial and inorganic, now looked like processions of saints bringing life and prosperity to the town.

Something fascinating is going to happen. I can feel it. The adventure I wanted is just around the corner. This is a place where those TV shows and comic books come to life.

His eyes sparkling with this misguided thought, Mikado found hope and excitement in his life ahead.

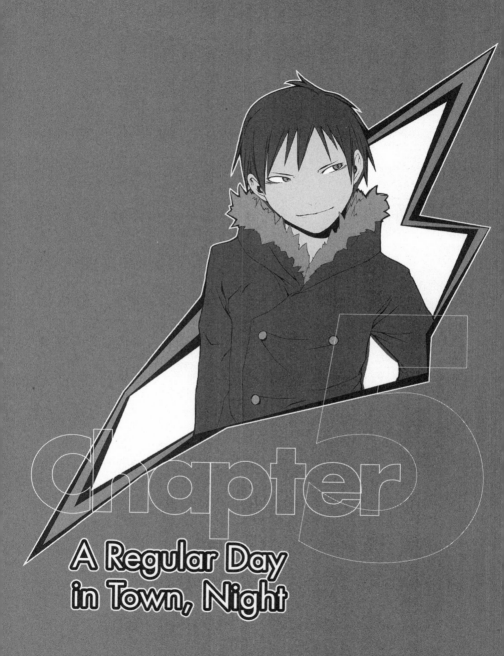

chapter 5

A Regular Day in Town, Night

"So anyway, is there anything in particular you'd like to do before you die?"

It was a rather frightening question for Izaya Orihara to ask in a karaoke room. He spoke calmly, drink in his hand, not bothering to choose a song.

But the two women he was asking just shook their heads without a word.

"I see. Are you sure you want to do this with me? There aren't better men you'd rather commit suicide with?"

"No. That's why we want to die."

"Good point," Izaya noted, his face still placid. He examined the two women. They didn't seem particularly gloomy. If a total stranger looked at them, they'd never suspect that these two harbored suicidal thoughts.

They had chosen to participate in a thread Izaya posted to a pro-suicide message board titled "Let's go through with it together!"

Izaya's message was extremely upbeat and positive, and for good reason: He'd taken a spam message from a dating site and tweaked the language a tiny bit, nothing more. But surprisingly enough, a quick perusal of the various posts on that board showed that many of them were optimistic in style. The text was crisp and practical, discussions of methods and motives for suicide, without any of the attitude one would expect a person preparing to die must exhibit. Some posts were as thorough as planning documents for a major business. Izaya enjoyed seeing the great variety of "invitations" on the site.

Of the two women here who had chosen death, one was having trouble finding a job. The other was in despair because she couldn't get over a broken heart.

Neither seemed to be a satisfactory reason to kill oneself, but such motives were proliferating since the beginning of the recession, and an aggregation of suicides grouped by career showed that the unemployed were easily the largest group. When grouped by age, suicides by those under the age of twenty were also far lower than any other age group. Because the media widely reported on those cases stemming from bullying or other youthful causes, there was a perception that many suicide victims were young, but the vast majority of them were actually adults. The two women with Izaya appeared to be in their midtwenties.

This was around the twentieth time that Izaya had met in person with the suicidal, and he was struck by how little he noticed in common among them. Everyone had their own way of approaching death—some couldn't stop themselves from laughing, and others couldn't stop themselves from setting up the DVR of their favorite show before they left to kill themselves.

However, none of the people that Izaya had met had ever actually committed suicide. And that was *very disappointing* to him.

The news ran reports on suicides. In recent years, the media picked up on cases where people had met online to commit suicide together. Because of that, the total suicide number was more than thirty thousand a year ever since.

What drove them to kill themselves? Did they have no other options? Were they prepared to die for the sake of others? How deep was the despair that surrounded them when they went?

Izaya Orihara loved people. Hence, he wanted to know them.

However, he wasn't meeting with these women in order to convince them not to die. The reason none of the people Izaya met had killed themselves wasn't because they were insincere looky-loos or were too afraid to die.

Beneath his calm exterior, Izaya's true nature flicked its tongue.

Izaya let them talk for a while, explaining their motives for suicide, but eventually he changed the topic with a bright question.

"So, what are you two planning to do *after you die?*"

Both women were momentarily stunned by this question.

"Huh...? You mean, like, heaven?"

They think they're going to commit suicide and get to heaven! How impertinent. This is what makes people so fascinating.

"Do you believe in the afterlife, Mr. Nakura?" the other woman asked Izaya. The name Nakura was just an alias he made up.

Izaya chuckled at their responses and shook his head, then turned the question back on them. "What about you? Do you believe?"

"I believe. Maybe there's no afterlife, but some people stay behind as ghosts to wander around," one of the women said, trailing off.

"I don't. There's nothing after you die, just darkness—but at least it's better than this," said the other. A giant red *X* popped into Izaya's head.

Ugh, what a letdown. What a terrible, terrible letdown. I've just wasted my time. What are they, middle schoolers? At least the last group were all atheists. They were fun. These ones are just drunk on themselves.

Izaya decided that these two were not taking the idea of death seriously. Or perhaps they were, but only in a way that suited themselves. His eyes narrowed, and he smiled with a hint of derision.

"Oh, come on. Why do you care what goes on after life if you're going to kill yourselves?"

"Huh...?"

The two women looked at Izaya in bewilderment. He continued softly.

"Believing in a world after death is a right reserved for the living. Either that, or you have to have done some major philosophizing about death. If that's the case, I've got nothing to say. Or perhaps if you're truly driven to the depths of despair or being hounded by unscrupulous loan sharks."

His calm, benevolent smile never wavered.

"In your case, that pressure is coming from the inside, isn't it? You can't just choose death because you're hoping the world after death is better."

At this point, the women realized that they'd spoken at length about their motives for dying, but the man with them had not spoken a word about his own situation.

"Um, Mr. Nakura…are you actually planning to die?" one of them asked, straight to the point.

Izaya didn't bat an eye. "Nope."

For a brief moment, the only sound in the room was the muffled bleed through from adjacent karaoke booths. Abruptly, one of the two women erupted, like a dam breaking.

"I don't believe this! You lied to us?!"

"Of all the… What a horrible thing to do!" the other added reprimandingly.

Izaya's expression did not budge. *I had a feeling they'd react this way.*

Izaya had been through this situation many times, and the reactions to his admission were, like the suicidal motives, wildly varied. Some people started swinging without warning, and some left without another word. But he didn't remember a single person who stayed entirely calm. Anyone who would respond to that admission with an easy "Oh, I see" wouldn't have sought suicide partners in the first place. Izaya didn't know every single human being, and the model of psychology didn't fit every person in the world, so he wouldn't state for certain—but he had a theory. If someone could remain perfectly calm through this, they were either cruising for kicks, or secretly wanted someone else to stop them, or were hoping to convince others not to commit suicide—or were *people like him.*

"What a pig! What's your problem? How can you do something so messed up?"

"Huh? Why?"

Izaya's face had the innocent wonder of an uncomprehending child. He looked back and forth between the two, then shut his eyes.

When he opened them again several seconds later, his delighted expression was gone, and a different kind of smile played across his lips.

"Aah…!"

The woman who claimed to believe in the afterlife sucked in a shrieking breath.

It was indeed a smile on Izaya's face. But this was an entirely different kind of smile. The two women, for the first time, learned that there were different types of smiles.

Izaya wore a smile as expressionless as a mask, and there was a coldness to it. It was the kind of smile that caused terrible fear in any who saw it, *because* it was a smile. In most cases the women would be hurling vile insults at him, but neither of them spoke now. They were grappling with the illusion that the other person in the room with them was not a human being at all.

Izaya repeated his question, not letting the smile fade from his face. "Why? What's so awful about it? I don't understand."

"Why? Because—"

"You girls," Izaya interrupted, his words harder than before, "have already decided to die. Why do you care what anyone says to you? The lies and insults are going to be gone forever in just a few moments. If it's torturous for you knowing that I tricked you, bite your tongue off. If you do that, it's not the blood loss that kills you. The shock causes the remainder of your tongue to compress your throat and suffocate you. Then all the bad stuff disappears. You will cease to exist. I think it's rather messed up of you to claim that I'm messed up."

"I know that! But..."

"No, you don't," he said to the woman who claimed there was no afterlife. His voice was even more forceful than before.

Still with a smile.

"You don't get it. You don't get it at all. You said there was nothing in the afterlife. But that's where you're wrong. Maybe you meant it in the sense that you won't have to suffer anymore—but death means to become nothing. It's not the pain that disappears, it's your existence."

The women did not argue back. They were paralyzed by the pressure of his smile. It grew more and more twisted, but the women still did not get a sense of the heart behind his words.

"The state of nothingness is not 'nothing.' Nothing is not always in contrast to 'something.' The nothing you speak of is eternal darkness, a blank slate. But that is as *perceived by you being aware of that darkness.* That's not nothing at all. If you're dying to be released from suffering, doesn't that require a form of you afterward that recognizes you've been released from suffering? You can't imagine that you're not even aware that you're not even aware that you're not thinking about this in the least. Fundamentally, there is no difference between the way both of you think. Even a grade school child who doesn't believe in life after death understands this and has feared and grappled with it."

In fact, Izaya's argument had plenty of holes in it, and the women knew they could argue back if they wanted. But their minds were ruled not by suspicion, but by terror—that no matter how they argued back, words would have no effect on this creature with them.

"But...that's...that's just what you think!" one of them boldly exclaimed, but Izaya's smile only devoured her words.

"Exactly. I don't know for sure. I just think that there's no afterlife. If it turns out that there is, hey, lucky me. That's as much as I care about this."

He laughed mechanically and continued, his voice even brighter than before.

"But you two are different. You only half believe in an afterlife. Does your religious sect promote the act of suicide and tell you that dying is a good response to career or romantic *failure*? If that's the case, I'm fine with it—I might even admit it's admirable of you. But if not, you should shut your damn mouths."

He raised his eyebrows and tilted his head as if seeking agreement, then leisurely uttered the finishing blow.

"You shouldn't speak of the afterlife when you only half believe in it. That's slander to the afterlife. It's an insult to those people who were driven to death by the evil intent of others when they didn't really want to die."

It was only a few seconds. But to the two women, it felt much longer.

In that brief, eternal moment, Izaya shut his eyes again—and when they opened, he was back to that original reassuring grin.

The air surrounding him completely different from just moments ago, Izaya changed the topic to something else, to the surprise of the paralyzed women.

"Ha-ha-ha, so anyway... When I was asking about your plans after death, I was referring to your money."

"...What?"

"I do hate for things to go to waste. Now, they're pretty strict about insurance claims these days, so that's ruled out, but you could go and borrow all the money you can, then give it to me before you die, right? Your deaths might be in vain, but at least your money won't be. Plus, there's a lot of value in your bodies and identities. I know where to go to make deals like that."

Unlike his terrifying smile from earlier, Izaya's current smile was warm and human. The things he was saying were faithfully, recognizably human in their greed. The women were about to speak, but once again, he cut them off.

"Question one: Why am I sitting in the spot closest to the door?"

Izaya was practically blocking the door in his current seat. The women were suddenly filled with a completely different kind of fear. If his previous smile was that of a devil, this one was concentrated human malice…

"Question two: What are these wheeled suitcases under the table for?"

The women had not noticed, until he pointed it out, that on the other side of the table from them were two large suitcases. They looked like the kind one would pack before a long overseas trip.

"Hint one: The suitcases are empty."

Both women were struck by an awful foreboding. They had never met before this event, but the similarity of their reactions to Izaya made them kindred spirits.

"Hint two: the suitcases are *just your size.*"

An unbearable nausea swept over them. It stemmed from disgust at the man with them, but the unexpected onset of dizziness was not related.

"?!"

"What…the…?"

By the time they noticed something was wrong with them, it was too late to even stand.

"Question three: If the two of you work together, you should be able to get past me to safety, so why can't you? Hint: I handed you your cups."

The world spun, spun, spun. Izaya's voice seized what remained of their fading wits. His soft, gentle coos and chirps ushered them into darkness like a lullaby to a baby.

"It's love. I don't feel any love in your deaths. And that's wrong. You must love death. You don't have enough respect for nothingness. And I'm not going to die with you after a sorry answer like that."

One of the women summoned the last of her strength to glare at Izaya.

"You'll never…get away with this! I'm going…to kill you…!"

Izaya looked happier than ever at this threat. He stroked her cheek tenderly.

"Good, very good. You can survive solely on that drive to hate. Pretty awesome, aren't I? I just saved your life. You owe me one."

Once they were both completely unconscious, Izaya put a hand to his temple and thought it over.

"Oh, wait. I'm not really into the idea of having a grudge hanging over my head. Maybe I should just go ahead and kill you anyway."

♂♀

Just before the clock struck midnight and changed the date, two shadows lurked in a corner of South Ikebukuro Park. One of them was Izaya Orihara—the other was an actual shadow.

"*So you just want to sit them on a park bench and leave?*" Celty typed into her electronic notepad—a PDA with a tiny keyboard.

Izaya read the message and cheerfully confirmed. He grinned and continued counting the stack of bills. "Normally I'd drag them to a loan shark and leech some money out of them, but I'm tired of all that."

"*Tired? You?*"

He'd hired Celty to help him transport two human beings. When she stepped into the karaoke box lobby, helmet still on, the employee simply pointed toward Izaya's room. On the other side of the door, Izaya was stuffing two unconscious women into suitcases. Before she could even type a pithy remark, he grinned and asked for help.

They'd hoisted their cargo all the way to the park, but Celty still didn't know anything about what had happened.

"I'm tired of it, and it's not a very efficient way of getting rich. The more it goes on, the more the police and mobsters will start looking into my activities. And this is only a hobby for me, not a job. Oh, thanks for helping on short notice. The professionals I usually ask were all busy. Usually I'd get a car to take them back to their parents, but with your motorcycle this is probably the best we can do."

Anyone who would take on this kind of job was probably not the good kind of "professional." Celty was not exactly pleased to be considered one of them, but she was used to it by now.

At least it ended quickly. It wasn't one of the jobs with a bad aftertaste. But not a good one, either.

"*Is this going to involve the police? I don't want to get dragged into something.*"

"Nothing you need to worry about. They're not bodies or anything. You just helped me escort two drunk women to a park bench, nothing more."

"*Inside suitcases?*"

Izaya ignored her jab, looking over the helmeted biker with great curiosity. Then he asked, "Hey, courier. Do you believe in an afterlife?"

"What's this all about?"

"Just humor me. Consider it part of the contract."

"You'll find out when you die," Celty typed irritatedly into her PDA, then added, *"How about you?"*

"I don't. So to be perfectly honest, I'm afraid of death. I want to live as long as I can."

"And yet you drug women for a hobby and sell information for a living?"

Izaya chuckled shyly. If that expression was the only thing to go on, he'd never be mistaken for someone fully immersed in the criminal underworld from head to toe.

"Hey, once you're dead, you're gone for good. It's a waste of your life if you don't enjoy it, right?"

Celty typed, *"You make me sick,"* into her PDA but deleted it before Izaya could see.

Izaya Orihara was an ordinary human being.

He did not wield extraordinary violence to evil ends and neither was he the kind of cold-minded killer who ended human life without compunction.

It was simply that he possessed both the greedy desire of a normal human being and the personal momentum to violate taboos if they stood in his way at the same time. He was not some charismatic mad villain, he just lived true to his interests. Because of that relentless pursuit of his "hobbies," he'd found a way to make a good living by selling information he picked up to organized crime or the police for cash.

But his name was known far and wide, and Izaya understood that. The kanji in his name were not typically read as "Izaya"—the name was a combination of Isaiah, the prophet in the Bible, and "one who approaches." He did not live a holy life fitting of the holy book, but on the other hand, he did exhibit an extraordinary capability to face new and different phenomena. That skill brought him to the life he now led.

He treasured his life as any normal person would, understood his limits, and spared no expense for his own safety. Thus, he had survived in the criminal underworld and was able to spend his days pursuing his interests.

Izaya left the rest of the chore to Celty, having fully enjoyed his first visit to Ikebukuro in weeks, and went home happy.

What had the women he met today looked like? How did they dress? Were they pretty, were they ugly, were they stylish, were they awkward? What did they sound like? Why did they want to die? Did they, in fact, even want to die? Izaya forgot all of these things.

Izaya Orihara was an absolute atheist. He did not believe in souls or the afterlife—which is why he wanted to know people. He found interest in others at the drop of a hat and trampled them just as quickly. When Izaya no longer needed to know a person, his lack of interest was absolute.

Barely ten yards from the scene, he had even forgotten the names of the two suicidal women. Unnecessary knowledge served no purpose to an information broker.

Two things were on his mind now.

One was the identity of the mute courier who always wore a helmet. The Reaper-like thing with the black scythe, riding a silent motorcycle.

The other was the group called the Dollars that had been at the center of rumors in Ikebukuro lately.

"I can't wait. I can't wait. I can't wait. Despite being an information agent, there's still so much of this town that I know nothing about being born and then disappearing. This is why I can't help but live here where all the people are! I love people! I just love human beings! I love 'em! Which is why people should love me back."

Izaya pulled his PDA out of his breast pocket. He turned it on, opened up the address book, and scrolled until he found the entry he wanted.

The name of the person was grandiose and ostentatious.

"Mikado Ryuugamine," the boy he had just met earlier that day.

Yagiri Pharmaceuticals, Upper Management

Somewhere between Ikebukuro and Shinjuku, in a location outside of the pleasure district of Mejiro, there was a quiet laboratory building. It was a three-story complex surrounded by fences and trees, the grounds quite spacious for Tokyo real estate, even when the long distance to the nearest train station was factored in.

This was the testing and research facility for Yagiri Pharmaceuticals, one of the elite corporations in that industry in the Kanto region around Tokyo. But the "elite" status was now a relic of the past, and the company's share was steadily shrinking with little sign of improvement.

Around the time their stock began slipping, an American business came with a merger offer. It was a conglomerate named Nebula, with a century of history behind it, active in shipping, publishing, and even biotechnology. Thanks to the bedrock of their business acumen, rumors abounded of unspoken understandings between Nebula and various politicians, but everything was kept secure through legal power.

For a merger, Nebula offered quite favorable terms that promised very little in the way of layoffs and restructuring, but some within the company—particularly the members of the Yagiri family itself, including the president—balked at certain conditions.

The most resistent member of the company was the young lab chief of the Sixth Development Lab, aka Lab Six, Namie Yagiri. She was only twenty-five years old and was the niece of the company president.

Her fast-track career course was not simply nepotism from her family's control of the company; her intellect and skill were exceptional. However, her blood was indeed a factor in her current position—not in terms of rank, but assignment.

It was the subject of that very lab that the Yagiri family secretly suspected was the driving force behind Nebula's merger offer.

Lab Six was not studying a new pharmaceutical, to be precise. On paper, it was developing new immune system substances for clinical trials...but what it actually contained was *not of this world*.

Twenty years ago, her uncle returned from an overseas trip with a taxidermy head that was modeled to look like a human's. It was as beautiful and still as if it were still alive, just sleeping. The pretty girl's head was tasteless, to be sure, but it was oddly tranquil, not barbaric. It seemed to anyone who looked at it like the head was an entire living thing all its own.

Though Namie did not know this at age five, the item had been smuggled into the country and would certainly have been seized at customs if declared properly.

Whatever the reason that her uncle had procured the head, it was treated like a Yagiri family heirloom. When he had time, he would lock himself in his study, gazing upon the head, even talking to it.

As a child, Namie visited that house often to spend the night with her cousin, and she found her uncle to be creepy, but that feeling faded over time as she grew accustomed to him. The only problem she had was that her younger brother, Seiji Yagiri, was even more attached to the head than her uncle was.

The first time Seiji saw the head was when he was ten. Namie snuck him into the study when their uncle wasn't around to show him the odd trophy. Even now, she terribly regretted this decision.

It was from that point on that Seiji slowly came undone.

He asked to go to Uncle's house more and more often. Whenever he could slip past Uncle's guard, he would stare at the head. With every passing year, Seiji's infatuation with the head grew stronger, until three years ago—the moment that Namie earned a job with her uncle's pharmaceutical company—he said to her, "I'm in love with a girl."

The girl her brother loved didn't have a name. Or a body below her neck.

The emotion that stole into Namie's heart at that moment wasn't the pitying sympathy for her brother's unrequited sexual fetish—it was the dark red and rusted flame of sheer jealousy.

Namie's parents were originally supposed to be next in line to inherit Yagiri Pharmaceuticals. But when Seiji was born, a large business deal went south because of a mistake on their part, and they lost face and authority within the company. After that, the love of their marriage went cold, and with it, the love of their daughter and son.

If anything, it was their uncle who offered more care and attention to Namie and Seiji. Their parents had no comment when they went to Uncle's house. It wasn't out of any implicit trust of him. They just didn't seem to care what happened.

On the other hand, their uncle's intention was to raise them as pawns of the family's interests. He cared for them as he would for his employees, not with the love reserved for one's family.

Eventually, Namie sought in her brother the kind of close family kinship that she was lacking elsewhere. That grew over time to eclipse the standard bounds of familial love into a twisted one-sided mockery of romance.

That was why Seiji's professed love for the head was so displeasing to her. Rather than returning the love she showed to him, Seiji chose to love a head, something that would never reciprocate his feelings. She knew that feeling jealousy toward a head was crazy, but she decided that she would sneak in and destroy it anyway.

But when she took the head out of the glass case, intending to discard it, the sensation on her fingers told her a terrible truth.

That soft skin was not the result of taxidermy. It had the warmth of any other person.

The head was *still alive*.

The years passed after that, and Namie convinced her uncle to let her study the head at the company lab. He informed her that this head belonged to a fairy known as a dullahan.

What a ridiculous story. Since when was a severed head a fairy rather than the usual winged human-bug things? But no matter the form it took, the important thing was that they had in their hands a being that transcended the normal concepts of life and death. This was a chance they couldn't let slip through their fingers.

Namie put the living head through a number of experiments. Half of her drive came solely from the jealousy surrounding her brother. She treated the thing as a "test subject" without remorse or reflection. She assumed that as long as the head was kept safely in the lab, Seiji would be unable to approach it.

The first problem was that Nebula contacted them as soon as she started the research. Despite the fact that the research team was extremely limited and tightly guarded, the American company's demands—complete control over the lab and its work—made it clear that they knew about the head.

Just when Namie was most paranoid toward the other members of the staff, fearing a traitor in their midst, the second incident happened. Her keycard, which she took home with her out of mistrust toward everyone else, was stolen.

The incident happened that night. Someone infiltrated the lab, used a stun baton on the three security guards, and took the head out of the building and nothing else.

What a colossal failure, Namie thought. *Everything's over.* But then she had an epiphany. She knew of exactly one person who was aware of the head's presence, desired it, and could steal the keycard from her...

But at almost the exact same time, she got a call coming from the apartment of the thief.

"Sis, I think I might have killed someone. What should I do?"

This cry for help came the night before Seiji's first day of high school. A girl who'd been stalking him had broken into his apartment and seen the head. He crushed her skull against the wall.

Namie did not feel terror at the fact that her brother had committed murder or anger that he had stolen the head—it was sheer joy she felt.

Her little Seiji was looking to her for help. He needed her. When she realized how much happier this made her than anything else in the world, she came to a firm decision.

She would protect her brother. Using any means necessary.

♂♀

【Do you know about the Dollars, Setton?】
[I've heard the name, but that's all. Weren't you talking to Kanra about this earlier?]
【Oh yeah, we did. I forgot, sorry about that.】
[No big deal.]
【A friend of mine was telling me about the rumors today. They sound pretty wild.】
[Hmm. I've never seen them in person. I wonder if they actually exist.]
【Meaning they could be nothing more than an Internet rumor?】
[I don't know for sure, but you could easily go about your normal life and never come across a team that you know for a fact exists.]
【I suppose you're right...】
[You ought to keep your distance from them anyway.]

—KANRA HAS ENTERED THE CHAT—
《Hiya! It's Kanra!》
【Good evening.】
[Evening.]
《What's this? Talking about the Dollars?》
《They do exist. They even have their own home page!》
《But you'll need a log-in and password to see it.》
【Ohh.】
[I wouldn't have any interest in seeing it anyway.]
【Kanra, you really do know everything.】
《Well, it's all I'm good for, lol.》

Chapter 7

Yagiri Pharmaceuticals, Under- Under- Underlings

Ikebukuro after midnight. A van was parked on the side of a road just outside the pleasure district. The rear windows were mirror tinted, with no way to tell what was inside.

In the midst of this zone of mystery, there was the sound of a hard impact and the pitiful shriek of a young man.

"I told you, I don't know! C'mon…please, give me a break!" the thug whined in an uncharacteristically polite tone, his face swollen and bruised.

This was the man who hit Celty with his car about twenty-four hours earlier and who had received a face full of scythe handle for his trouble. When he came to, he was inside the back of this unfamiliar van, arms and legs tied up. There were no seats in the back of the van, just gray carpet. There was another man there with him, who had been asking the same question since he came to his senses.

"Like I asked, who's giving you the orders?"

Three seconds of silence would earn him a punch. Claiming ignorance would earn him a punch. There would be a brief recess, then the process repeated. This had been going on for three hours.

Even in the midst of this beating, the thug was able to calmly and rationally analyze his situation.

I don't know who this guy is, but at least I know that shadow isn't here.

On the other hand, I don't even know if these people and the shadow are connected in some way.

The only people in the van with him were the large man who was beating him and another man in a hat, chewing gum in the driver's seat. The van's stereo was playing classical music at medium volume, loud enough to keep most wails from attracting notice outside.

If that shadow was here, I'd be screwed. I might have panicked and told it everything. At least this guy's a human being, not a monster like last night. In fact, it would be way scarier to have someone higher up in the organization kill me than these guys. I'm just lucky I didn't get caught by the cops. Whoever these people are, I'll be fine if I just don't tell them who hired me. As long as I can keep taking these punches, they'll eventually figure I really don't know anything. I mean, they're not crazy enough to kill me.

The man in front of the thug sighed.

"C'mon, just spit it out already. Look, we've got bosses, just like you do. I don't need to tell you what I mean, do I? And they're real concerned because you guys have been pulling this stuff without telling them about it."

Great, so there are mobsters behind this guy. Dammit, I thought we cleared things up with whatever yakuza owned that territory!

"But since you're not giving up a name at this point, you're not yakuza. If you were, you'd be contacting whatever yakuza you work for to settle the situation. People above our pay grade on both sides would hash the issue out. But since you're not doing that, it's something else that's backing you, isn't it?" he chided, lifting the thug's chin with a finger, as though he were scolding a naughty child.

Essentially, if the thug they held in this van was a member of some backing organization like an organized crime syndicate, they couldn't get rid of him themselves. But the fact that he wasn't identifying himself meant that either he was afraid of being held responsible for this failure by his bosses—or whoever he was affiliated with wasn't a yakuza or foreign mafia.

"Look, I'm saying this out of consideration for your situation. If you know what's best for you, you'll speak up and—"

The van's side door slammed open.

"Well, well, was today a scorcher or what?"

"Thanks for waiting! Well, how'd it go, Shimada? Did he talk?"

A man and woman climbed into the rear of the van without asking. The woman was dressed in brand-name fashion, and the man was well dressed, too, though for some reason he was carrying a bulging backpack.

The man named Shimada looked over at them and sighed sadly.

"Nope, outta time. You get the consolation prize. I feel sorry for this schlub, but he's yours now, Yumasaki."

He gave one last pitying glance to the thug, then left the van. The new man and woman closed the door after Shimada left, then turned excitedly to the thug.

"Boy, you really screwed up big time, pal. You just had to be the one who kidnapped poor Kaztano," the woman said, patting him on the shoulder.

Kaztano? Who? That sounds familiar, the thug thought. As a matter of fact, it was the illegal immigrant he'd kidnapped yesterday. *Of course, these must be his people. But wait, they're Japanese. How are they related? Surely they're not in some kind of teatime club.*

The sharp-eyed man lowered his backpack and unzipped it before the confused thug's eyes.

"Well, well, well. We hear you haven't spilled your secrets yet, so we're gonna need to use some special tools."

He pulled several books out of the bag.

"It's the eleventh anniversary of Dengeki Bunko. You know the motto: Feel the lightning! So pick a book, any book. We'll torture you in some way related to that book. Normally we give a choice of super-robot anime, but since we picked up a whole bunch of Dengeki Bunko novels today, this is your selection. Ha-ha-ha!"

"Eh?"

It was less his intentions that the thug found confusing than the words he was speaking. The man spread out a number of novels plastered with colorful illustrations. Then again, given that the thug never read any book that wasn't manga, he mistakenly assumed that they must be comic books.

What the hell is this? Torture? What do you mean, pick a book? Is that a joke? What do you think this is, the school bus?

"No, no, no. You have to choose…or I'll just kill you."

The man's eyes were bright and smiling, but there was no deception in them. Bolstering the threat was the presence of a silver hammer that had somehow appeared in his hands.

The thug immediately decided that his best course of action was to choose a book that seemed the least painful.

Dammit! How can this be happening to me? What about Gassan and the others? Argh, just gotta pick one... Well, I know I definitely don't want to pick this Bludgeoning Angel Dokuro-chan. *It's got a pretty girl on the cover, but I can guess what that involves based on the title. What about...*Double Brid...V? *Wait, that kid on the cover has a bandage on his head. More bludgeoning? Damn, aren't any of these normal...?*

"Personally, I'd recommend this one: *Inukami!*" the girl piped up, and the guy agreed.

"Ooh, good choice! But which one, *dai-jaen*? *Shukichi*?"

"*Shukichi*'s better for midday. I dunno, should we just go with *Dokuro-chan*?"

"Nahh, it's too big of a pain to recreate Excalibolg..."

??? What are they saying? Are these gang names?!

The thug was completely at a loss. The man and woman were muttering unfamiliar words like strange curses. Apparently, he wasn't the only one left out of the loop. The man in the driver's seat with the sharp assassin's eyes chewed his gum loudly, clearly irritated.

"Yumasaki, Karisawa. Listen up—I ain't much for reading, so I don't know what the hell you're talking about, but I have one suggestion," he said, as though coming to a sudden realization. "Go ahead and have your fun, just don't use gasoline inside the van like last time."

"Aww, you're no fun, Togusa," grumbled the man, picking up several of the books.

Gaso—?!

Things were clearly worse than the scenarios he'd been imagining. The thug was losing his grip on the situation. Now there was no way to tell which of the books remaining promised the least painful torture. Upon further thought, no matter what the content of the books were, these people were clearly crazy enough to make up something gruesome.

"C...can I ask you just one thing?"

"Mmm? What is it? And no asking what the torture will be—I have a no-spoilers policy!"

"If...if you had a book of Cinderella and I picked that one, what would you do to me?"

The man stopped to think, then patted a fist into his palm.

"I'd grind down your feet with a file until they could fit into glass slippers."

I knew it! They'll find a way to make anything awful!

The thug closed his eyes and grabbed a book at random. It had an English title, with the Japanese reading in small letters next to it, and was adorned by a delicate illustration.

"And the choice is made!"

"Wow, you've got some stones, pal. Quite a gutsy choice!"

The man and woman showed an unnerving ease with their preparations. She took a hand mirror out of her bag and handed it to him. He immediately cracked the mirror with the hammer and placed a few of the shards in his palm.

"I wonder how many pieces of mirror we need to be able to see things that should be invisible? Time to test it out!"

Meanwhile, the woman held the thug's head still and forced his left eyelid open. Suddenly he understood exactly what was going to happen to him.

"W-w-wait! You're kidding! You can't do this to me! Stop...stop!"

"Kids, don't try this at home. But who would ever try this anyway?" Yumasaki warned, his face growing more serious by the moment.

Karisawa cheerily injected, "Is this one of those moral panic things about people killing because of the influence of manga?"

"No, no, no. Let's make this clear for the benefit of our delinquent friend here—there's nothing wrong with manga or novels. They cannot speak for themselves, and the blame for a crime always falls upon the silent, you know?"

The thug begged and pleaded for mercy with tears in his eyes as the two prattled on with their inane references. The man ignored the cries and slowly but surely brought the pointed shard of mirror glass closer to the thug's exposed eyeball.

"Manga and novels and movies and video games and our parents and our school have nothing to do with this. If there's any reason we do this, it's because we're just plain crazy. If there were no manga or novels, we'd base this on a historical play, and if not for that, we'd use some classic old Natsume Soseki novel or something else approved by the Ministry of Education. And what would the politicians say about us then?"

"Nnnooooo-aaaaahhh!"

"Besides, anyone who says they did it because of the influence of manga wasn't a true fan to begin with."

Just as the pointed tip of the shard was about to sink into his eyeball, the thug's spirit of salvation appeared.

"Knock it off."

The rear door of the van suddenly opened and a heavy, brusque voice filled the interior.

"Dotachin!"

"K-Kadota!"

The man and woman both straightened up, their eyes wide. This new person was clearly a superior rank. The man named Kadota glared at the thug up and down, then looked at the would-be torturers.

"That's not how you torture someone. Also, don't get blood on the books, you clown."

"S-sorry."

Kadota grabbed the thug's collar in one hand and lifted him up. The thug's breathing was an irregular mix of heaves and sobs, his eyes, nose, and mouth glistening with a mix of tears, snot, and drool as he desperately attempted to calm himself down and regain control.

Kadota simply said, "Your pal talked."

"Uh...wha...whuh?!"

At first, he didn't understand what Kadota meant, but as it gradually sank in, the thug's face cycled rapidly through a stream of emotions.

I've been sold out?! Who did it?! Gassan? No—but who—damn— what's going on—we're completely ruined! What's happening out there?!

"We've only got part of the story so far, but in time, we'll know the entire truth. Which means we don't actually need you anymore."

If they didn't need him, they might let him walk. That was perfect. If he was just going to be erased by the people from his *own company*, at least this way he had the option of disappearing on his own and laying

low. Despite the confusion, the thug finally began to feel a faint hint of hope. Then, Kadota put that hope to rest for good.

"So now you can die with a clean conscience."

Everything inside of him crumbled into ruin.

"Wait a sec! I mean, w-wait please! I'll talk...I'll tell you everything! Whatever you want to know! I'll tell you whatever they didn't say yet! Just please, please, please don't kill meee!"

"I see. So despite the sinister getup, you're actually just a salaryman, technically speaking."

According to the thug, they were hired by a small temp agency to do various utility jobs. But that was just for outward appearances—in fact, that temp agency was part of a larger, different company.

That company was a pharmaceutical producer, recently down on its luck, with headquarters and a lab complex in Ikebukuro.

Kadota grinned happily at the thug's story. "So a corporation in financial trouble is kidnapping people for human experimentation? And this is happening in a first-world country?"

He sounded skeptical, but in reality, he didn't doubt the thug's story. It was hard to imagine him being able to lie at this point, and there were plenty of rumors around Yagiri Pharmaceuticals already.

Kadota told them to let the thug out at a random spot, then started to leave the van.

In a frail voice, the thug called out to his back.

"Who...who are...you people...?"

Kadota stopped and answered without turning back.

"...If I said we were the Dollars, would that ring a bell?"

Once Kadota was out of the car, Shimada called out to him.

"Um, Kadota, when you said the other guy talked...were you lying?"

"You could tell?"

Shimada looked exasperated for a moment, then grinned.

"Look, I just didn't want to let Yumasaki do his thing. I like those Dengeki Bunko books. It pains me to see them making a mockery of those stories."

"...Oh. Kinda funny, this is the first time we've ever done something like this as the Dollars. I mean, we decided to go ahead and do this for Kaztano's sake, but if it weren't for the Dollars, we'd never have met him to begin with..."

Kadota, Shimada, Yumasaki and Karisawa were all members of the same organization.

At first it was just a clique of good friends, but eventually Kadota found that some downright dangerous people like Yumasaki were joining in positions below him. He didn't know what he'd done wrong to cause this, but now that they were affiliated with him, he needed to keep them under control. As time went on, though, he failed to find any of them jobs, and now everyone aside from Kadota was simply bouncing around between part-time gigs.

They knew some other folks on the wrong side of the law, but as the group didn't have the backing of any major gangs, they mostly stayed out of trouble—until one day their leader Kadota received an invitation. It simply asked if they wanted to join the Dollars.

No restrictions, no rules, they just had to call themselves Dollars. It was a very weird invitation. Neither side seemed to benefit from this, but the Dollars were making a name for themselves around Ikebukuro and the label seemed prestigious. Kadota himself was not that interested, but the rest of the group was all for it, so he eventually gave in.

It must be my easygoing nature that caused this. Hell, even Shizuo Heiwajima has a regular job.

At first he thought it was just a prank pulled by someone who knew his e-mail address, so he accepted just to play along, but the very next day, his handle name appeared on the Dollars' home page.

"So what's the Dollars' boss saying about this one?"

"No idea."

"Huh?"

"That's the trouble. I've still never seen the leader of this gang. We've got this hierarchy of all the little groups the Dollars have absorbed, but I can't find whoever sits at the top."

Kadota couldn't help but wonder who actually created this bizarre organization. He didn't like working for someone whose name or face he did not know, but on the other hand, without a clear boss, he didn't really feel like he was working for anyone in the first place.

If anyone would set up something like this, it would have to be—

Izaya Orihara.

He used to live in Ikebukuro, and Kadota had met him on several occasions. The man rudely stuck him with the nickname "Dotachin," and Karisawa still called him that.

With the unexpected appearance of that name in his mind, and the realization that imagining a nonexistent leader didn't do him a bit of good, Kadota decided to put it all out of his mind.

The true powers in this town were the yakuza, the foreign mafia, and the police. If anything, the Dollars ranked well below them.

No matter how much they captured the imagination, their numbers and power meant nothing in the end—a fleeting illusion in the shifting midst of the city.

And that was exactly why he wanted proof that this illusion really existed.

But Kadota understood.

Only after the illusion vanished would he really know if that's what the Dollars were.

Double Heroine,
Sonohara

Chapter

Several days of high school formalities passed for Mikado, and after the customary health inspection, actual classes were scheduled to begin the following day. At Raira Academy, the opening ceremonies happened on the first day of school, the second was reserved for an introduction to the school's clubs and activities, and the third was for health inspections and homeroom.

In the midst of the aforementioned post-inspection homeroom, the class decided on who should be their committee representatives.

"I know, let's go pick up chicks," Masaomi suggested in the manner of a commercial slogan, smacking his textbook shut.

Masaomi was in Class B, and yet for some reason he was hanging out in Mikado's Class A. Considering that the majority of students were in uniforms, his personal clothes made him stand out even more.

"What are you doing here?" Mikado finally asked, though he'd noticed Masaomi's presence minutes earlier. There was no teacher present, so the boy in seat number one was carrying out the proceedings in his place.

"So Mr. Yamazaki and Ms. Nishizaki will be our Beautification Committee members, and Mr. Yagiri and Ms. Asakura will be our Health Committee reps, while Mr. Kuzuhara and Ms. Kanemura are on the Discipline Committee, and for the election monitor…"

It was standard practice for one male and one female student to be chosen for each committee. The proxy leader read aloud each of the selections written on the blackboard, then considered what was left.

"So we're still missing our class representatives. Any volunteers?"

"Ye—"

Masaomi tried to raise his hand, but Mikado grabbed it and pulled it down.

Class rep. It seems cool, but it might also be a pain in the ass.

What Mikado wanted was an escape from the doldrums. He'd already flown from the familiar sights of his hometown to an exciting new city, and emboldened by the experiences he'd had over the last few days, his desire for thrills was stronger than ever before.

Mikado's brain, stimulated by the excitement of a new city, couldn't help but ignore the risks and scream for more.

More chills, more abnormality, more revolution!

Mikado was in such an elated state of mind that he would have fallen for any scams, ripoffs, or cults out to target him. He wouldn't have thought twice about an invitation from Masaomi to a motorcycle gang meetup.

Despite his unquestioning mind-set, Mikado had enough self-awareness to know that while the special rank of class representative promised new experiences, he also didn't want to be tied down to too much responsibility.

Maybe it's best if I just sit back and let this play out...

"..."

One girl raised her hand, her eyes downcast.

It was Anri Sonohara, pale and bespectacled. The beautiful but aloof girl surrounded by an aura that said to stay away.

"Umm, Miss...Anri Sonohara? Let's put her on the board, then."

A very disinterested round of applause rose from the class. No one else seemed particularly engaged in the question of who would take what position.

"I'll let you handle the rest, then," the temporary leader said, writing Anri's name on the blackboard and retreating to his seat.

"In that case, is there anyone who wants to be the male class representative?"

Her voice was frail but clear. No one volunteered for the position, and an uneasy silence fell upon the classroom.

What should I do? Mikado wondered as he gazed in a trance at Anri behind the teacher's desk. Suddenly, her glance fell upon one of the male students.

Mikado followed her eyes until he saw a particularly tall classmate. He was the second tallest in the class, and Mikado recognized him as the one who'd just been elected to the Health Committee.

Seiji Yagiri. That was the name written on the blackboard beneath the Health Committee heading. Aside from his height, nothing about him seemed out of the ordinary. But there was almost nothing boyish left in his face—if he'd been introduced as three years older, it could have been taken at face value.

But if he was already assigned to a committee, why was the girl named Anri staring at him like that? Mikado began to wonder if she might have a thing for him, when...

Her gaze shifted directly to Mikado's direction.

Huh?

Behind her glasses, Anri's facial expression suggested concern. Mikado's heart leaped a beat.

"I'm a sinful man," Masaomi muttered jokingly the moment Anri's eyes shifted away. "She's totally got the hots for me. She's feeling anxious about the wild, dangerous night ahead of us."

It was spoken quietly enough that only Mikado could hear. He decided to shoot back a barb of his own.

"Sorry, can you speak Japanese? This is Japan, after all."

"Damn! Always with the quick comeback! I never realized the danger in my midst was coming from you, my old friend—but I live for the sake of love and won't hesitate to kill a pal if I must."

"No hesitation in the slightest?!"

Upon more levelheaded reflection, she might have been looking at the outsider Masaomi rather than Mikado. That might explain the worry he saw. Which raised the question: What was Masaomi doing in that seat anyway?

That's when he realized what she was *really* looking at.

The seat Masaomi was occupying belonged to a female student

who hadn't appeared in any of the last three days, starting from the entrance ceremony. He recalled that Anri had been concerned for that student during that very first day.

Mikado silently raised his hand. He had no idea what was running through Anri's mind, but if no one else was going to volunteer, it might as well be him.

"Oh...um..."

"It's Ryuugamine. First name, Mikado. Meaning 'imperial man,'" Masaomi interjected for some reason. Anri dutifully wrote the name on the blackboard. Several members of the class finally noticed Masaomi's presence, but no one seemed particularly concerned. No use ruffling any feathers—and nobody really wanted to get involved with an unknown student wearing his own clothes, with bleached brown hair and earrings.

In a way, Mikado's plain appearance and subdued personality made him fit the role of class rep quite well. No one raised any objections, and the process continued uneventfully.

"Well, that's all the positions—don't forget to attend your first committee meetings tomorrow. The times and places are written on the board outside the office," the new class rep read off the printout on the teacher's desk, bringing a quiet close to the homeroom period.

"We can go ahead and leave after cleaning up. Let's get to it."

In the end, Mikado became a class rep without even standing in front of the class. He started on the cleaning process, feeling slightly unfulfilled. As he mopped the hallway floor, Masaomi teased him, leaning against a window.

"Aha, so that's what's going on..."

"What do you mean?"

"I didn't think you had it in you. Back in elementary school, you'd cry just because someone made up rumors about you and a childhood friend. And somehow you've turned into an aggressive hunter on the prowl, looking for love!"

"Oh, that. Whatever," Mikado muttered, brushing off his friend's nonsense. "Speaking of which, did you join anything?"

"Yep, the Discipline Committee."

Mikado tried to imagine his friend being in charge of student behavior. He summed up his thoughts with one word. "Yikes..."

"What do you mean, yikes? Hey, I actually wanted to be class rep, but we needed a ferocious fifteen-man rock-paper-scissors tournament to decide that slot, and I was tragically eliminated."

"Fifteen volunteers?! In a rock-paper-scissors competition?! Geez, your class was way more into it!" Mikado blurted, openly astonished. Masaomi grinned in satisfaction.

"But there were only six volunteers for Discipline. I dunno about that guy from your class, though; he looks like a real stickler for discipline. I'm hoping to use my position on the inside to tear down the system from within."

"...What are you talking about?"

"Whatever. Now that I'm on the Discipline Committee, there are no heavy firearms coming onto this campus!"

"But small firearms are okay...?" Mikado murmured, having regained his cool head.

Masaomi stomped his leg with cartoonish disappointment. He looked out the window for a few moments, then turned back with a sense of purpose.

"I know, let's go pick up chicks!" Masaomi repeated.

"Seriously, are you okay?"

Mikado finished up his cleaning assignment, feeling concern for the old friend who was getting more and more unhinged by the day. He placed the mop in a large storage locker and picked up his bag, walking off with Masaomi—when he noticed Anri Sonohara at the entrance of the building with the tall shadow of Seiji Yagiri. Anri was asking him something, her face dead serious, while Seiji looked annoyed.

"—Then——so it's——really——seen her?"

"I told you, I haven't. She just stopped coming."

Anri's words were too quiet to make out accurately, but Seiji's irritated answer was plenty clear. He turned in the direction of the two boys, clearly hoping to brush Anri off. He was in charge of cleaning the entranceway, so his bag was probably still in the classroom.

Anri watched him retreat, then noticed Mikado and Masaomi staring at her. She hastily walked out of the door.

"Whoa, whoa, no need to be putting on a show with this quarrel on the third day of school, young lovers," Masaomi said. Mikado turned to see that he was already blocking Seiji's path. The combination of his words and appearance made Masaomi the perfect villain for this scene.

"...What do you want? That wasn't what you think it is."

"Umm, you're Yagiri, right? I'm in the same class as you. Mikado Ryuugamine."

"Yeah...I remember you. Hard to forget a name like that," Seiji said, his tension easing as he recognized his class representative. Mikado had stepped in between the two to prevent anything from erupting, but Masaomi pushed him aside to get closer.

"Hey...Kida!"

"You're pretty fit, dude. Let's go pick up chicks!"

"Huhhh?" both Mikado and Seiji interjected.

"Kida, what in the world are you talking about?"

"It always helps to have one really tall guy in the group when you go cruising! If it were just you and me, it'd be a zero-sum game—every positive effect of my appearance would be canceled out by the negative effect of yours."

"That's mean! Why don't you just invite someone from your class?"

"You idiot, if I did that, I'd have like twenty boys and girls coming along!"

Mikado was about to ask why girls would be tagging along for a pickup run when Seiji interrupted. He was no longer irritated the way he was earlier, though he didn't seem to be in a mood to listen to the other two bicker, either.

"Sorry, but I've already got a girlfriend."

That ought to have been the clincher, but Masaomi was not to be deterred.

"As if that matters!"

"Uh, yes it does!" Mikado interjected, but Masaomi paid him no attention.

"I don't care about the presence or absence of any girlfriend—just talking to another girl doesn't make her your girlfriend, so there's no issue of cheating whatsoever!"

"Huh? Really?" Mikado asked, momentarily swayed by the flood of

Masaomi's logical barrage. Seiji was unaffected in the slightest, however. He simply shook his head quietly.

"No way. Even thinking about another girl is an act of betrayal."

"Well, aren't you a bastion of integrity? So you can't possibly betray your girlfriend?"

"It's not my girlfriend I'd be betraying."

"Huh? Then who?" Masaomi asked.

Seiji looked into open air, his eyes full of light and purpose. "Love."

"Pardon?"

"I would be betraying the love I send to my girlfriend. I could betray her, but I can't betray my love."

Silence.

"Uh…okay, dude."

An uncomfortable pause enveloped all three, but Seiji's expression didn't change in the least. The glory of belief and certainty shone in his eyes.

"Well, um…good luck with that!"

Masaomi offered him a hesitant fist, and Seiji bumped it back with a brilliant smile.

"Yeah, thanks!"

He headed off to the classroom without another word. Masaomi watched him confidently stride away and muttered, "Looks like you've got a real hothead in your class, too."

"I guess you're right."

♂♀

"This is pathetic."

They were at the famous Ikebukuro West Gate Park—as seen on TV!—but for the middle of a weekday, it was virtually barren. Mikado had absolutely zero intention of playing along with Masaomi's flirtation mission, but he was interested in taking a closer look at the place he'd seen on television so many times.

It was indeed the locale he recognized, but Mikado soon realized that seeing it in person was a completely different experience. The location was the backdrop for news broadcasts, TV dramas, and variety shows, but each program gave it a different feeling.

Impressed with how editing and presentation could create such different impressions of the same place, Mikado watched Masaomi do his thing. It was exasperating.

Masaomi couldn't find any high school girls his age, so he had to resort to hitting on the office ladies who walked through the park on their lunch breaks. Of course, no working adult (on their break) was going to sit around and entertain the advances of a teenage boy. The sight of his desperate, futile attempts was kind of touching in a way.

When Mikado relayed this to Masaomi after he took a short break, his friend grinned and replied, "What do you mean? The goal is just to talk to women, and I'm succeeding with flying colors! Besides, calling things desperate or futile is the *last* thing you should do when talking to women! When you're around a beautiful woman, the only thing that ensures your actions are desperate or futile is thinking that they are. You get me?"

"I don't get you at all," Mikado muttered and stretched lazily. There was no point to just sitting around here all day, so he decided to head somewhere he wanted to go. "I'm going over to 60-Kai Street on my own."

"What? You think you can pick up chicks without a wingman? When did you turn into such a lady-killer?"

"I'm not going to pick up chicks."

But Masaomi wasn't listening. He jabbed a finger at Mikado's face and leered, "You're going to be reduced to tears over the loss of my skills soon enough! You're gonna wind up getting played by one of those *ganguro* girls who don't realize that the overtanned look was out of style years ago!"

"What does any of that have to do with your skill?!"

"Shut it, shut it, let your mouth be a door and *shut it*! Let's have a competition! We'll see who can pick up more girls, me or you!"

"Seriously? You're gonna hit on girls while trailing an entourage of girls you hit on?"

Masaomi ignored him and started sprinting toward the station. Within moments, he was calling out to a housewife with her child and shopping bags.

Mikado let out his deepest sigh of the day and headed to the east exit of the station on his own.

It wasn't a perfectly straight line, but he did manage to reach 60-Kai Street with relative ease. This point actually wasn't that far from his apartment. Mikado planned to wander around checking out stores until nightfall, then head straight home. If Masaomi was still the same person Mikado remembered from elementary school, he'd forget about the silly competition and go home soon.

When they were seven, Masaomi was "it" in a game of hide-and-seek, and he left to go home in the middle of the game. When Mikado finally returned home that night in tears, Masaomi was there in the house. With his cheeks full of Mikado's dinner, he said, "Found ya."

Now that I think about it, we had our share of adventures back in that town. I wonder when those stopped happening.

There was nothing particularly interesting to relate from middle school. It was just a very long succession of safe, boring days.

Mikado dreamed of the outside world but had no reason to leave his hometown. He'd been stuck in an unchanging situation—until the day his family got an Internet connection, and his world changed forever.

Now there were endless worlds at his fingertips. He had access to information he would never learn from his ordinary life. It was as though, just on the other side of the world he lived in, a much, much larger world had appeared. And in the new world, there was no such thing as distance.

As he delved further and further into the world of the Net and found himself on the verge of living a shut-in existence, Mikado one day came to an epiphany. He was free to passively receive anything and everything from the Internet—but when it came time to add his own information to that world, there was almost nothing he had to say or share.

When he realized this, Mikado became even more fascinated with the world outside of his town. The picture of Tokyo that Masaomi painted for him shone brighter than ever before.

And now he was within that light. Masaomi claimed that the

countryside was where it was brightest now, but Mikado didn't get that feeling yet. He knew what his friend meant, and he didn't intend to leave and never look back. But he knew that when nostalgia did register, it would be further on in the future, not now.

Mikado just wanted to savor the taste of the big city and breathe in its air so that it infused with his lungs.

As though he were a part of the city itself.

He spun around to take in more of the scenery and that city air.

Raira Academy uniforms filled 60-Kai Street, and the town itself seemed to be dyed with the color of the outfit.

"They're almost their own color gang," he muttered, then noticed a familiar face. "Sonohara!"

He was about to walk over to her when he noticed that she was surrounded by other girls in the same uniform, and there was a prickly tension in the air. They were close to the entrance of a side alley where it met the street, and the three girls had Anri pinned against the wall.

Curious, Mikado carefully approached the alley. None of the four girls noticed him, but he was close enough to make out every word of the conversation. In fact, it was less of a conversation than a one-sided interrogation.

"I hear you think you're some kinda big shot even without that Mika Harima around."

"..."

"And now you're the class rep? What are you, some kinda goody-goody?"

"Why don't you say something? You were like a barnacle stuck on Mika's side in middle school."

The three girls were taking turns verbally abusing Anri, but she showed no sign of reacting to any of it.

Are they seriously bullying her? Do people in Japan still do that?! And those insults are so...clichéd! It's like they walked out of an old manga!

Mikado found it hard to be intimidated by such stereotypical insults. As a fellow class rep, he knew he ought to step in—but his brain was hung up on the idea of what he should actually *do*. It wouldn't really work to pretend he didn't see anything now, but he also didn't like the idea of getting on the girls' shit list.

I know! I'll walk up with a smile and say, "Why, fancy meeting you here, Sonohara," as if I don't realize she's being picked on! Yes, that's the plan! And if those girls say anything, I'll think on my feet.

His idea seemed trapped somewhere between optimism and pessimism, but Mikado was already walking forward...when a hand caught his shoulder from behind.

"?!"

He held his breath and turned around to see a familiar face.

"Stepping in to stop the bullying? Very brave," said Izaya Orihara, looking interested. He kept his grip but started pushing Mikado forward instead of pulling.

"Uh, what?!" Mikado shrieked, finally drawing the attention of the four girls.

"H-h-hi, Sonohara, wh-wh-what a c-c-c-coincidennnn— Aaaa— Hang on!"

Izaya pushed him right into the midst of the girls.

"Wh-what's the big deal?" asked one of the bullies, somewhat intimidated. It was meant not for Mikado, but the man behind him, of course.

"You really shouldn't be extorting people out in broad daylight like this. God might let you get away with it, but the police won't," Izaya joked. He continued to approach the girls. "Bullying really is the lamest thing you can do."

"Like it's any of your beeswax, old man!" the girls screeched, either because they had finally shown their true colors or as a bluff to hide their fear.

"You're right, it's not," he said, grinning. He delivered the three girls a warning. "It's none of my business. If you're beat up and left here to die, that's none of my business. If I decided to assault you, if I decided to stab you, if you decided to call me, a twenty-three-year-old man, "old," it would not change the fact that your affairs and mine are eternally unrelated. Every human being has a connection to every other, and yet we are all unrelated."

"Huh?"

"Human beings are so vapid," Izaya said enigmatically and took another step toward them. "Look, I'm not really into the idea of hitting girls."

In the next moment, a small bag appeared in Izaya's right hand.

"Huh? What?" one of the girls piped up, recognizing the expensive-looking bag. Somehow it had made its way from its customary spot on her shoulder into the man's hands. The strap, still hanging over her shoulder, was cut clean at the waist.

While the girls were thrown into confusion, Mikado was downright terrified.

In Izaya's left hand, held behind his back, was a very sharp knife. The scariest part was that Mikado had been watching the man's movements the entire time, but he never noticed where the knife came from or when he'd slashed the bag free of the strap.

Izaya smartly folded up the knife and slipped it into the sleeve of his suit jacket, all one-handed behind his back. Mikado felt like he was watching a magician at work.

Still grinning, the older man pulled a cell phone out of the little bag.

"So I think I'll start a new hobby—stomping on girls' cell phones."

He tossed her phone into the air. It clacked and clattered on the ground, the case plastered in little stickers.

"Hey, what's the big—?"

She quickly reached out to pick up the phone...

And Izaya stepped hard on it, just barely missing her outstretched fingers.

With the sound of crunching snacks, broken shards of split plastic appeared under the sole of his shoe. The girl shrieked in horror, but Izaya stomped again and again. The movement was mechanical and precise, hitting the exact same spot over and over. The robotic repetition even extended to his laugh.

"Ah-ha-ha-ha-ha-ha-ha-ha-ha-ha-ha-ha-ha-ha-ha-ha."

"Oh my God, I think he's *on* something!"

"What a creep! Let's get outta here!"

The other two dragged off the victim of the phone stomping, who looked on in mute shock. They exited the alley onto the main street and disappeared.

Once he was certain they were gone, Izaya's laughing and stomping stopped instantly. He turned to Mikado as if nothing had just happened. Anri did not run, but stayed where she was, watching Izaya and Mikado with fright in her eyes.

"I'm bored. I think I'm over the phone-stomping fad," Izaya said and gave Mikado a gentle smile. "It's pretty brave of you to help someone being bullied. Most kids these days wouldn't do that."

"Oh…?"

Anri looked at Mikado, surprised. Given his extremely weak and passive attempt to help, and the confusion wrought by Izaya's grand entrance, Mikado seemed to be trying to forget he'd done anything.

Unperturbed by any of this, Izaya addressed the boy slowly and deliberately.

"Mikado Ryuugamine, our meeting was no coincidence. I was searching for you."

"Huh?"

Mikado was about to ask what he meant by that when a trash can from a convenience store hit Izaya square on the side.

The trash can fell in place, crashing to the ground with a tremendous clattering.

"*Guh!*" Izaya grunted, losing his balance and falling to his knees. The metal can hit him straight on, but the impact was from the flat side rather than an edge, so the damage wasn't as bad as it sounded.

Izaya lurched to his feet and glared in the direction the trash can had come from.

"Sh-Shizu."

"Iiizaaayaaa," came a lazy voice. Mikado and Anri slowly turned toward it.

It was a young man with sunglasses. He was wearing a classic bartender's outfit with a snappy bow tie, like an old-fashioned solicitor for a cabaret club or a hostess bar. The man was quite tall, though not as tall as Simon. But his frame was lithe and compact, not the body of a man you'd expect to throw a trash can that far.

"Didn't I tell you never to show your face in Ikebukuro again, Iiizaaayaaa?"

Izaya very clearly recognized the man, and for the first time in Mikado's presence, the smile vanished from his face.

"I thought you were working over toward the West Gate, Shizu."

"I got fired ages ago. Plus, I told you not to call me that, Iiizaaayaaa. How many times have I told you that my name is Shizuo Heiwajima?"

the man growled, veins pulsing on his face. His features were ordinary enough that he looked like a typical bartender by default, but the invisible aura of domination he emitted tipped Mikado's scales from intimidation straight into terror.

I've never actually seen someone with bulging veins in real life before, Mikado initially thought, but in moments his body was completely controlled by primal, instinctual fear.

Shizuo Heiwajima—one of the people Masaomi said never to mess with. He had qualified that with "outside of yakuza," so at the very least, this man was an ordinary civilian. But Mikado felt with all of his being that if there was a person who lived through violence alone, this was him.

It all made sense. Virtually any person living in Japan, upon seeing this man, would know they didn't want the first thing to do with him. It would be easier to avoid him with a face that screamed danger from a distance, but it was his very ordinary looks that made him so dangerous.

"Come on, Shizu. Are you still mad about me framing you for my crime?"

"I'm not mad at all. I just want to beat your brains in."

"Oh, c'mon. Just let me go."

Izaya pulled the knife out of his sleeve. "I don't like your violence, Shizu, because it doesn't respond to reason, words, or logic."

"Aaah!" Anri shrieked at the sight of the silvery blade, finally snapped out of her daze. Mikado held his breath and tried to motion to her to run away. She nodded, her back pressed to the wall, then clutched her bag to her chest and raced away. Mikado followed right behind her, turning back just once to glance down the alley.

Shizuo's bellow of rage echoed off the walls, and people on the sidewalk stopped and looked down the side alley. Then, parting the crowd, the enormous shape of Simon, well over six feet tall—and Mikado couldn't watch anymore.

Absolute terror swirled within him. His new city was a maelstrom of the ordinary and extraordinary, but he didn't know which of the two this was. The only thing he knew was that he must never get involved with whatever that was.

He finally understood what Masaomi meant by the people to never make enemies with.

And those are regular civilians. How terrifying must the yakuza and Chinese mafia be?

The tales of violence he read about on the Net seemed like they had to partially be just that: tales. Now that he'd come into direct contact with it himself, Mikado was overwhelmed by the fear that actual violence inspired.

Finally, he gauged that it was safe, and he called out to Anri.

"H-hey, w...wait...hurts to...breathe..."

Sadly, even though he was running with all of his strength, he never once broke ahead of Anri.

That was the cruel shackle of reality as Mikado Ryuugamine knew it.

"Are you all right?"

Mikado took Anri to a nearby café, hoping to calm her down. He ordered them two cream sodas, then later realized it seemed like a childish choice.

"Um... Thank you for your help."

"Uh, n-no, not at all! If anything, it was that Izaya guy who saved you!"

"But..."

Damn, what should I say? This just had to happen when Masaomi isn't here to help me out.

Mikado wasn't sure what to do, but he knew that not saying anything at all wasn't an option, so he tried to find a topic.

"So...were those girls from your middle school?"

Anri nodded.

"That explains it. So when you were in middle school, this Mika girl was there to stick up for you when they bugged you, but now that she's gone, those bullies from the past seized their chance to get back at you?"

Anri trembled at Mikado's conjecture. "H-how did you know that?!"

"Um, j-just a guess based on the conversation... Anyway, is this Mika the Mika Harima from our class?"

She seemed to be calmer now and started to explain. "The thing is... Mika's been marked absent at school, but in fact, she hasn't been home at all since the day before the entrance ceremony."

"...Huh?"

That seemed like a matter for the police. The concern must have shown in Mikado's eyes, because Anri quietly shook her head.

"Technically, she's not missing—she's been sending e-mails to both my cell phone and her family. Messages like, 'I'm going on a journey of spiritual healing.' Or a report of whatever train station she's currently at."

"Spiritual healing? What happened?"

"Well, uh..."

For the first time, Anri was unable to answer. She cast her eyes down, clearly not wanting to talk about it.

"Don't worry, I won't tell anyone. The guy who *would* talk is too busy having an affair with a housewife right now," Mikado blabbered while insisting on his ability to keep secrets. Anri failed to notice the contradiction. She thought for several moments.

"Will you promise not to be shocked?"

"Oh, nothing could shock me after the scene we just witnessed," Mikado said, putting on his most reassuring smile. The time he spent with Masaomi in elementary school had taught him the proper way to soften a situation for the other person.

That boyish smile apparently did the trick, because Anri put it as bluntly as possible.

"Mika Harima...is a stalker."

Plurfp!

Half-melted ice cream spurted out of Mikado's smiling mouth.

Once her story was done, Mikado tried to piece it together.

"I see... So Yagiri the Health Committee rep was being bothered...er, romantically approached by Mika, and when he turned her down, she went on a journey of healing to fix her broken heart?"

According to Anri, Mika Harima had a habit of doing this, going back to middle school—picking the locks of the homes of boys she fell in love with at first sight or researching their vacation destinations and meeting them there, only to thank them for inviting her. In short, she changed the truth to whatever suited her.

On top of that personality, she had excellent grades and a rich family.

She got her own apartment to live in while at high school, one with a monthly rent of more than 100,000 yen. Raira Academy had its own dorm, but it was located so far away from the school campus that most students chose to commute from home or got their own apartments to learn independent living at a young age. Mikado was one of the latter, as was Anri, who had a cheap place a little farther away.

This Harima girl's got quite a life.

Then she met Seiji Yagiri and decided that he was The One. She started visiting his home, then failed to show up for the first day of school. According to Seiji, he gave her a very convincing no on the day before the entrance ceremony, warned her that he'd call the police—and hadn't seen her since.

Mikado felt a cold sweat forming as he heard more and more of Anri's story. Apparently she'd been sitting between him and Seiji during the school's entrance exams. It could very easily have been Mikado whom Mika had decided to follow. He was secretly relieved that he hadn't saved any girls in town so far—not that he would've been able to if he wanted.

He didn't let any of these thoughts cross his face, though. Mikado was all business as he listened to Anri's story.

"So what happens when you call her?"

"She won't pick up... It seems like she keeps her phone off except to send messages... When I brought that up in an e-mail, she said she didn't want to hear my voice because it would make her homesick..."

"I see... Hmmm. I wonder if it's best to just hang back for now... Or maybe, just in case, you could put a little pressure on her in a message by saying you might have to call the police if you don't hear her voice?"

Mikado tried a number of commonsense suggestions, but none were solid opinions of his. Time dragged on without an apparent solution.

"By the way, would you say you're her best friend?"

"...I can't say for certain, but we were together all the time. I'm a bit awkward and don't know how to get along with people, and she was the one who took me by the hand and pulled me along. After that, we were always together..."

Mikado suddenly realized that the two girls were not just simple friends. One heard stories about this on the Internet, where the beating heart of such friendships was always spelled out in the most gruesome, harsh terms.

"Plus, with her grades, she could have gone to a much better school than this. Instead, she chose to go to mine. I felt really bad about that..."

That's probably because she thought you were a useful tool and foil for her and didn't want to lose you...

Mikado just barely kept that sentiment from reaching his lips. He was very glad that Masaomi wasn't present. If this conversation was happening in a chat room, he'd have blurted that out without a second thought.

But maybe making that clear would ultimately be the best for her, Mikado thought, his eyes wandering as his mind grappled with indecision.

Anri noticed this and giggled. "It's okay, I know the truth."

Shocked that he was so easy to read, Mikado stammered a hasty "Wh-what?"

"I know that I was nothing more than a foil for her. And to be frank, I was using her as well. I don't think I could survive without doing that. The reason I volunteered for the class rep job was because I knew she'd want to do it. So I figured if she wasn't able, at least it should be me."

Now everything made sense to Mikado. When Anri looked his way during homeroom, it wasn't him she was looking at—it was Mika's empty seat. Only it wasn't empty because Masaomi was occupying it.

Meanwhile, Anri revealed some information he hadn't asked her for.

"But, in fact, it's just for my own self-satisfaction. I felt like, if I can be the class rep, I might even be able to surpass her... I think it's very unfair of me."

Before she could finish her thought, Mikado cut in, his voice cold and clinical. "Actually, the worst part of it is that you're telling someone else."

"..."

"It's like you're hoping that someone unrelated to the situation will forgive you for your actions. At least trying to be better than her in some fashion is the right choice. So you should hold your head high and do it fair and square."

Inwardly, Mikado chided himself for taking it too far. After their long conversation, he'd gotten so engaged that he ended up telling her something he would normally have kept to himself. He watched her reaction, half-afraid she would explode with anger—but she seemed neither angry nor upset.

"Yes, I suppose so... Thank you," she smiled sadly.

Mikado thought to himself, *How pretty must Mika Harima be if she's using this girl to make herself look better?*

It was probably more of a foil for personality than for looks, but Mikado couldn't help but wonder.

"Um, thank you very much."

Anri bowed to Mikado again as they said good-bye. Mikado wanted to pay for their order at the café, but she insisted, and they split the bill. The shadows were stretching long across 60-Kai Street, and the deepening sky silently stared down at the two.

"No, it's okay. This was the first time we ever talked, but now that we're the representatives of our class, I guess we'll be seeing a lot more of each other."

Anri smiled kindly and nodded.

"Actually, Ryuugamine, I've known about you for a while."

"Huh?"

"When I came to deliver my enrollment form to the office, they checked it against a list of names. I spotted a cool-looking name on the list, and no sooner had I noticed it than someone came and checked it off..."

Something weird was happening. Mikado gave her a bland affirmative, trying to dispel the feeling of dread welling up in his chest.

"And now...the owner of that very name has helped me out of a bind."

Just a second.

It was starting to sound exactly like the situation between Mika and Seiji. Anri was smiling at him, her face a mask over her true intentions.

Uh, crap. I don't think I'm ready for a stalker... But would it be so bad if it was a really cute girl like her? Yes, it would. What if she ends up stabbing me?! Or she might set my house on fire or take my family hostage... But if it turns out she's cool, then I wouldn't mind her stalking me... Wait, no! If she's a stalker, that rules out the possibility of being cool entirely! Then again, if I really had to choose yes or no...

After three seconds of wild, circular speculation, Mikado realized he had no idea how to react to his classmate.

Anri noticed his discomfort and giggled. "I'm joking."

"Uh..."

"I'm sure you don't want someone like me hanging around and bothering you. But don't worry, I'm not a stalker."

Along with the realization that she was teasing him, Mikado felt a deep shame at having been so obvious—as well as an even greater sense of guilt.

"...Sorry."

"Huh? N-no, don't apologize! I'm the one who was teasing you!" Anri stammered, wide-eyed, clearly not expecting an apology.

They both cast about awkwardly for something to say, and Mikado broke the silence with a simple "Well, see you tomorrow."

"Yes, I suppose we'll be seeing plenty of each other."

She might have a bit of a sneaky streak to her, but she's a good person at heart, Mikado thought as he headed back to his apartment. She wasn't the otherworldly spirit he originally imagined, just a normal girl with an awkward life.

Maybe it's kind of like my relationship with Masaomi. He's the one who always tugs me around, and it's how I came into contact with my new world here.

Mikado shook his head, reminding himself that he shouldn't be thinking that way. Instead, he remembered the girl named Mika Harima, who had disappeared after her crush rejected her advances.

"He must have really shut her down hard. But if that's all it took to make her give up, maybe she wasn't that bad of a stalker to begin with," he mumbled to himself.

Then again, according to Anri's story, Mika had picked the lock of her crush's apartment—while she was in middle school. Would she really give up on her "man of fate" because of a little police threat?

Mikado realized he was spending serious thought on a stalker he'd never met. He rolled his head back to the sky and sighed.

I know I was hoping for some wild stuff to happen, but not these disappearances and stalkers.

He swallowed his melancholy and stopped walking, hoping for a change of pace. Maybe he could find a hundred-yen shop to browse through on the way back home.

A sound that bridged reality and fantasy hit his ears.

An engine rumble like the whinny of some living animal. It groaned and growled in fits and starts, sounding more agitated than ever before.

"The Black Rider!"

Mikado couldn't stifle his rising curiosity and excitement—he never expected to hear the bike so close to the crowded station. He raced off in the direction of the sound.

Just one turn at the next intersection and it should be in view. He tried not to let the moment take control of him, pulled right around the corner—

And into a scene from an old-fashioned manga.

♂♀

"...Oh ho. So you ran into a beautiful girl rounding a corner, and she just so happened to be running from a bad guy on a motorcycle, plus she has amnesia. And you want me to accept each and every one of those details at face value."

"What can I say? It's all true."

"If there's one thing amongst all that truth that doesn't make sense, it's the mystery of why she ran into you around that corner instead of me."

Mikado and Masaomi were arguing in the midst of a cramped apartment room measuring just four and a half tatami mats—less than a hundred square feet.

Mikado's new apartment contained no other appliances than a PC with onboard TV tuner and a rice cooker. It was one of the cheapest rooms in his building—the only one cheaper was the three-tatami room next door. It was only because that spot was taken that Mikado had to take the more expensive option. But apparently that tenant was a cameraman who was typically out on location, so most days it was empty.

He felt he could have taken that tiny room, but now that he had a guest over, he realized just how small four and a half already was and thanked God that he hadn't tried for a three-mat room given the current circumstances.

Unlike Mikado's wild confusion over said circumstances, Masaomi was calm and cool.

"Now, it would have been really trite—er, tight—if you were running late for school. It would have been marvelous if she turned out to be a new transfer student to your class. And it would have been perfect if she was a queen from a far-off country…and your long-lost childhood friend to boot!"

Mikado rubbed his chin, completely ignoring Masaomi's ideas.

I know I asked for the extraordinary, but this much of it makes me wonder if it's all a dream. I hope it's a dream.

Masaomi continued goofing around, despite Mikado's silence.

"Did you pick up on that pun with trite and tight?"

"There's nothing less funny than explaining your own joke."

Mikado looked down at the girl lying next to them, feeling like he had just said that not long ago. He couldn't tell how old she was, but she looked older than him. She slept in total peace, wearing plain pajamas that looked like they came from a nearby hospital.

When they collided just around that corner, she asked him for help. He stood there in confused disbelief until he noticed a black motorcycle was heading straight for them.

The rest he did not remember. Apparently he grabbed her by the arm and pulled her into the train station. The motorcycle couldn't follow him down there, and they left from a different exit, then ran to Mikado's apartment.

"It sounded like she lost her memory, and she said not to call the police…so I didn't know what else to do…"

"Just have to wait it out, I guess," said Masaomi, watching the sleeping girl. "She is beautiful, though. Almost doesn't look Japanese… In fact, *is* she Japanese?"

"Well, she was speaking Japanese…"

They decided that waiting until tomorrow to ask her more was the best plan. Normally, the circumstances dictated that such a person be turned over to the police for help, regardless of what they said, but Mikado had no intention of doing that.

Yes, it might be a well-worn development, but it was still a scene right out of a movie or comic book. This was the exact kind of adventure he wanted.

The only thing that caused him concern was the fact that the Black Rider might now be able to recognize him. He'd grabbed the girl and safely gotten away, but he still had no idea why the black motorcycle would be chasing her. If he had to survive in the big city knowing that the urban legend Black Rider was after him...

He hated normal, boring stuff. He wanted a different life than the one regular people had. Perhaps that was why he'd chosen to harbor this mysterious girl.

But escaping the ordinary required the assumption of risks.

Was the Black Rider my risk?

Mikado's imagination set him shivering as Masaomi said good-bye.

There was one thing Mikado kept secret from his friend.

A bandage was currently wrapped around the girl's neck. It hadn't been there before Masaomi came over to visit, but once Mikado got a good look at her, he noticed something very striking.

Below her head, *in a clean circle running completely around her neck,* was a series of needle marks resembling medical stitches.

As though a saw had taken her head right off, and someone had sewn it back on.

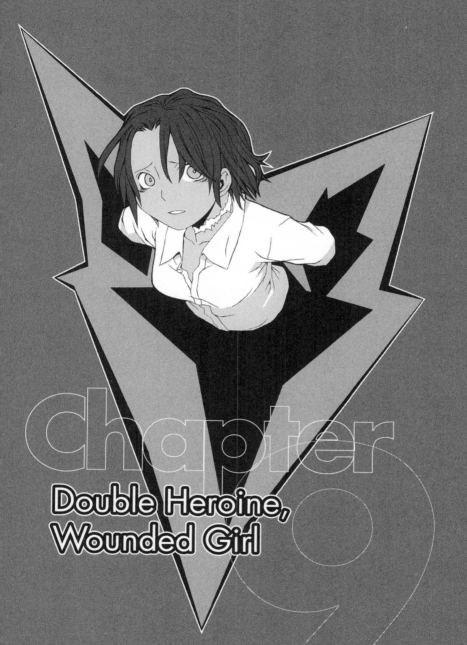

Chapter 9

Double Heroine, Wounded Girl

We rewind the clock.

Right around the time that Mikado and Anri walked into the café, a "pawn" elsewhere in the neighborhood lurched into motion.

Research lab, Yagiri Pharmaceuticals

A dull thud echoed off the walls of the Lab Six meeting room.

"What do you mean…*escaped*?"

Coffee streamed across the table out of the tipped cup next to Namie Yagiri's clenched fist. The scalding liquid burned the skin of her hand, but she didn't bat an eye. Her fist trembled only with quiet rage and panic.

"If the police find out, we're done for! All of us!"

She scanned the faces of her subordinates, anger and haste glittering in her eyes.

"So you played nice and quiet while you were looking for your chance to escape…"

Eventually she bit her lip to hold the rage inside. Her tongue was painted a darker red than just from her lipstick.

"…Very well. I want our full street-level forces in action. No more skulking around in the shadows now, use every possible resource— and if any trouble arises, have it taken care of promptly."

"Shall I order them not to harm the target?" asked one of the men at her side.

Namie thought it over briefly, then gave the order in unequivocal terms.

"It would be quite a shame—but in this case, I want our property returned, dead or alive."

♂♀

Seiji Yagiri sighed as he made his way to the research lab where he would find his sister.

Yes, this is love. A love that cannot be stopped.

Seiji first met "her" five years ago. As a ten-year-old boy, his sister snuck him face-to-face with his uncle's secret.

"She" was like a sleeping beauty in a fairy tale, waiting for the arrival of her Prince Charming within that glass case. Despite the grisly appearance of a severed head, Seiji felt not the least bit of fear or disgust. His boyish heart was completely bewitched by the majesty of the object.

As he grew older, Seiji developed reason. But his sense of reason originated from, and revolved around, her head, and she eventually ate away at his mind. The head did not cast a conscious spell on him, nor did it use some kind of brain waves or pheromones. The head just *lived*. And in the act of staying true to his heart, Seiji Yagiri fell completely in love with her.

Just as Namie Yagiri looked to her brother for love, that brother sought love from a mute head. And that pure desire spurred him into motion.

When his sister took the head away under the guise of research, Seiji thought, *I want to set her free from the prison of that glass case. I want to show her the world.*

He believed that she would want it that way and waited years for his chance to strike. He stole his sister's security card, memorized the patrol guards' routes, then knocked them out with a stun baton. Seiji felt no guilt—he only wanted to see the joy on her face. But even after taking her out of the lab, she did not wake.

The head did not return his love. But that was because his love was insufficient, he told himself. Thus did Seiji continue to believe that his utterly one-sided infatuation was in fact an eternal bond.

Why does love once gained and then lost feel so dear? Seiji lamented, like some preteen in love with the idea of love, as he strode toward the laboratory with severe purpose.

"I know I told sis to handle it...but I just can't let *her* be alone in there. Plus, it's just too cruel to cut open her head and peer inside, even if it is for the sake of science," he muttered to himself, completely unaware of the dire nature of events. Seiji passed through the entrance doors of the lab.

"I shouldn't have given her back. I should have fought and argued. As long as I show them the truth of my love, sis and Uncle will understand eventually. And if that doesn't work, we can just elope."

They were the words of some star-crossed nobleman hoping to marry a commoner, but there was no hesitation or doubt in Seiji's intent. By all appearances, he seemed to be a perfectly normal, optimistic teenage boy—but that very ordinariness turned horribly, grotesquely wrong when his love interest was revealed to be a living, sleeping head.

Even worse, however, was the fact that the entire existence of Mika Harima was completely, permanently gone from his mind. She had impacted him directly, but he could no longer recall her face or the sound of her voice. As an obstacle to his love, Seiji had eradicated all traces of her from his memory, and a man who lived on love alone had no need to recall the obstacles he had eliminated.

If I have to, I'll just steal her keycard again, Seiji thought as he watched a cleaning van race out of the laboratory's parking lot.

Seiji knew they were not cleaners, but the so-called "underlings" of the lab: kidnappers doing its dark bidding. And not kidnappers involved with slavery rings in some far-off country, but the kind dealing with illegal human experiments.

On top of that, Seiji knew that they got into this abduction business because of their research on her. They ran experiments on the kidnapped victims using the cells, genetic data, and even liquids they extracted from her. It baffled him why they needed to go to these paranoid, urban legend lengths to study an actual head that really existed, but it probably had to do with the pressure being put on Yagiri Pharmaceuticals by that Nebula company. At least, as far as Seiji understood it.

Apparently the experiments were not cruel, grisly vivisections, but conducted after using anesthetics to put the subjects into a coma. Once they got the data they wanted, the victims were released alive in a park or some other location. They would choose victims that couldn't otherwise go to the police about their abduction—illegal immigrants or criminal types without the backing of one of the powerful mobs—but there were also rumors that the underlings would kidnap runaway girls and other lucrative targets to make their own money on the side.

The bastards make me sick. Have they no respect for human life?

Seiji glared at the van as it passed, filled with a righteous anger—then noticed that someone was stuck to the rear door of the van.

The thing—no, the person—clinging onto the back of the vehicle had a scar running around her neck.

And above that scar—was the head of his dearly beloved.

The lightless motorcycle sped down the street outside the train station without a sound.

It passed directly in front of the police box, but the officers did not notice the dark, silent vehicle. At worst, the occasional pedestrian looked on in confusion at a motorcycle emitting no engine sound. It was trying to stay relatively inconspicuous in that very public location, so it wasn't reckless—if anything, the rider was careful not to let its darkened bike cause other vehicles to collide. When it did speed up, it let the engine roar a tiny bit, just to alert the people around it of its presence.

The headless horse—the Coiste Bodhar—could frighten people with its roar, and that had not changed since its spirit had been transferred to a motorcycle, but occasionally it had the opposite effect, drawing the excited interest of onlookers instead. Despite her alarm at the varied nature of the humans around her, the dullahan had learned how best to ride through the town over the years. She just didn't realize that she had become the stuff of urban legend.

When she didn't have any work, Celty wandered around the town searching for her head—but naturally, she never just happened across a severed head lying on the ground, so it was an essentially meaningless activity. The dullahan understood that perfectly well, but she couldn't stand the idea of just sitting around doing nothing, and so she wandered.

To her surprise, she had seen essentially *zero* fairies or spirits aside from herself since coming to Japan. On very rare occasions, she might sense the tiniest sliver of something from the trees lining the center of a park or along the entrance to 60-Kai Street, but she had never seen them for herself. She had felt many more of her kind back in Ireland. Celty thought it would be better to have another dullahan along to help her look for the head, but that was out of the question now. Twenty years later, the security around ship stowaways and smugglers was far stronger. It would take the presence of that very head of hers to leave Japan at this point.

It eventually dawned on Celty that it might be completely impossible for her to find supernatural entities like herself within the limits of her abilities here.

That's just the world of man for you. I suppose it would be the same in New York or Paris. Perhaps if I looked in the forest of Hachioji...or just traveled all the way to Hokkaido or Okinawa, where there's more nature...

But without her head, she could not travel anywhere without Shinra's help. There was only so far a person could go wearing a helmet without drawing extra suspicion.

Besides, she couldn't leave Tokyo until she had found her head. What if she left for a different region now, and when she came back, that faint sensation she'd followed here was gone for good?

By checking the locations that she could no longer sense the head against a map, Celty knew that wherever her head was, it was centered in Ikebukuro. But without a way to narrow that down to anything more specific, her only option was just to wander around the area in search of it.

Ultimately, that search was in the form of a simple type of street patrol. If she found something curious, she looked it up on the Internet, and anything more suspicious than that required the help of Shinra or Izaya to identify. That was the best she could do.

So perhaps unsurprisingly, she had gained no hints whatsoever in twenty years.

Facing another day of undoubtedly useless searching, Celty heard Shinra's words echo inside of her heart.

"Just give up."

That wasn't an option. She wasn't exactly unhappy with her life as it stood now, but in order to stifle the feeling that swirled within her, she needed to find true tranquillity. She needed her head back.

The light turned red, and Celty came to a silent stop. As she waited, a figure at the side of the intersection called out to her.

"Yo, Celty."

She looked over to see a man wearing a bartender's outfit. It was Shizuo Heiwajima, whose name meant "Quiet Island of Peace"—or, as Shinra called him, the "guy in town who least lives up to his name."

"Can I talk to you for a sec?"

Celty had been patrolling Ikebukuro for twenty years, and for much of that time, she'd known this man. Of course, he had no idea of Celty's true nature or her gender, but Shizuo was also the kind of man who didn't bother with little details like that. When the light turned green, Celty turned left and pulled over to step off the bike.

Shizuo's clothes were ripped here and there, as though slashed by a knife. He had probably just been in a fight.

If anyone could have cut up Shizuo's outfit like this, it was probably Izaya Orihara. Sure enough, that information came straight from the horse's mouth in seconds.

"Izaya's back here in Ikebukuro... I was just about to sock him a good one, but Simon stepped in to stop me in the nick of time."

Based on just that statement, Shizuo was indeed a laid-back, well-behaved person. But that was only because Celty never talked.

Shizuo snapped at the tiniest things. He got irritated and angered over words, so the more talkative a person, the quicker he became enraged. She'd seen Shinra and Shizuo have a conversation once, and it was as tender and tricky a situation as handling a stick of dynamite with the fuse lit.

He especially hated people who argued in logical circles, and thus Shizuo and Izaya Orihara were always at odds. For his part, Izaya hated people that his logic didn't work on, so the two of them kept antagonizing the other.

Until Izaya moved to Shinjuku, the two fought on 60-Kai Street nearly every day, until Simon broke up their brawl and forced them into his sushi shop, each and every time.

As a parting gift when he moved away, Izaya framed Shizuo for several crimes and was crafty enough not to attract any attention to his part in them.

After that, their rivalry was set in stone, and trouble always followed whenever one visited the other's neighborhood. "Trouble" meaning simple fights, of course, but Izaya was clever enough to maneuver such that they never got the police or yakuza involved.

"Unlike Kadota or Yumasaki, when I get into trouble I'm always alone. I think the same goes for Izaya. He doesn't have any friends or partners. Which isn't to say that I don't get lonely myself. I want to have connections to other people, even if it's only going through the motions."

Celty nodded to show the grumbling brawler she understood.

A bartender in sunglasses and a shadow wearing a helmet. It was a surreal pairing at a glance, but the people around them barely did more than look and showed no signs of interest.

Shizuo had clearly been drinking, probably at Simon's sushi place. Celty felt it would be cruel to just leave him hanging, so she let him speak his mind for a bit, until…

"What I want to know is, *what's Izaya doing back here*?"

Celty knew the answer to that question. Ikebukuro was simply the setting for Izaya's latest twisted interest. But there was another detail weighing on her mind.

The strange thing is that he was here for two days in a row.

Izaya's base for his information brokerage business was in Shinjuku. He wasn't the kind of man with time on his hands every day. If he was hanging around, especially with Shizuo's presence, he had to be doing so with a specific purpose in mind.

"Now that I think about it, I'm pretty sure I saw him speaking to some kid from Raira Academy…"

Shizuo stopped in the middle of his thought. He looked through the crowds.

"What's that?"

Celty turned to view the surrounding area. Amid the mass of people coming and going, a number of them were watching a specific person. Right at the center of those gathered gazes was a single woman.

On the street behind them was a woman in pajamas, probably in her late teens, tottering through the sunset on uncertain legs. Perhaps she had been hurt, or perhaps she just escaped from the clutches of some of the city's unsavory residents.

Celty had no desire to draw extra attention, but given that someone's life might be hanging in the balance, she let herself focus on the woman anyway.

And froze on the spot.

It was her face as she remembered it from the water surface or the reflection of windows.

Hair as black as darkness, just tracing over her eyes, features that were carved into her heart long in the distant past—right atop the shoulders of the woman stumbling across the sidewalk in her pajamas!

Celty's emotions exploded. She raced forward. Shizuo followed her over to the woman, curious. She grabbed the unsteady woman by the wrist and forcefully turned her for a better look. The woman swallowed in shock, then shrieked madly, trying to undo Celty's grip.

"Ah... *Aaaah, noooo!*"

The crowd turned its attention on Celty, but she was too agitated to notice. She only wanted a better look at the woman's face, but the situation was too chaotic to pull out her PDA for a message now.

"Uh, please calm down. We're not here to hurt you," Shizuo said helpfully as he approached. He put a hand on her shoulder, hoping to calm her down.

Thukk.

A shock ran through his side. Something felt very wrong around his thigh, just below the buttock, sending both cold and heat into his pants.

"Wha...?"

Shizuo swung around to see a young man wearing a school blazer, crouched down and stabbing something into Shizuo's thigh.

It was an ordinary office-use ballpoint pen, the kind one would find anywhere. The boy's bag was half-open—he must have pulled the pen out of that and stabbed it into Shizuo's leg.

"What...?"

"Let go of her!" the boy shouted.

Celty turned to see what this new disturbance was, noticed the sudden bloodshed, and stopped in her tracks.

Sensing an opportunity, the girl in the pajamas tugged herself free of Celty's grip and started running down the street. Celty moved to follow her but held up at the last moment, looking back. Shizuo was standing there with two pens jammed into his thigh, while the young man in the blazer was pulling out a third.

The crowd burst into worried murmurs, several of them falling back in panic. Some affected a mix of nonchalance and fear, trying to skirt around the crowd as though nothing was happening, while others just walked straight through the scene in complete ignorance. Some even pulled out their phones to snap pictures. There were two police boxes in the vicinity, but the situation erupted directly between both of them, and it would take a three hundred–yard run to reach either one.

With a brief glance at the crowd, the young man in the blazer looked in the direction the girl in pajamas went, his third pen still in hand.

Then he muttered, "Thank goodness…"

Celty was going to demand what he meant by that, but Shizuo thrust out a hand first. His palm snapped to a halt right before the edge of her helmet, and he smiled as though nothing was wrong.

"I'm fine. Too drunk to feel much pain. You go after her. I don't know what's going on, but you need to follow her, don't you?"

He folded up his sunglasses and tucked them into his shirt pocket, then smacked his own face.

"Ha-ha! Always wanted to say that one. 'I'll handle this. You go on ahead!'"

That line was usually reserved for when the enemy was unfathomably strong, and if anything it was the student boy whose life was now in danger—but Celty decided to indulge Shizuo rather than worry about the young man's well-being. Besides, if she stuck around and they got caught by the police, she might be able to explain that Shizuo was the victim, but she wouldn't be able to explain who she was.

Celty put her hands together in apology, then straddled her bike to chase after the girl. People in the crowd exclaimed in surprise at the Black Rider's presence in their midst. Her trusty steed roared high, drowning out the onlookers as it echoed throughout the night city.

"Stop!" The boy in the blazer tried to chase after her.

"That's what I'm saying." Shizuo grabbed the boy by the back of his collar and dragged him backward. "Is that your girlfriend?"

"Yes! She's my soulmate!" the boy—Seiji Yagiri—stated with absolute confidence, flailing wildly in an attempt to escape.

"Why is she like…that?" Shizuo asked, still entirely calm.

"I have no idea!"

"What's her name?"

"How the hell should I know?!"

The crowd, watching at a distance, felt a sudden chill. The man in the bartender's outfit, who had seemed relatively normal and nice, now had veins bulging on his face. The warmth drained out of the air.

All of that heat sucked out of the surrounding space was added to his rage—and Heiwajima exploded. "What the hell is that?!"

The young man flew.

"No way!" the crowd shrieked.

Without a shred of hesitation, Shizuo *tossed* Seiji's body directly into the street. He slammed into the side of a delivery truck that was waiting at the light. If the light had been green, Seiji might easily be dead in seconds. Even more shocking was the sheer distance for one human being to throw another. Every person watching the scene sucked in a freezing breath.

"Isn't it just a liiittle irresponsible, not even knowing your girl's name? Huh?"

Seiji's bounce off the truck landed him back on the sidewalk. Shizuo walked over and grabbed him by the collar again, pulling him up to chest level.

But even numbed by that powerful shock, Seiji met Shizuo's monstrous glare with a powerful gaze of purpose.

"Names don't matter...when you're truly in love!"

"Huh?" Shizuo glared at him even harder, but Seiji did not falter in the least. "How do you know she's your soul mate when you don't even know her name yet?"

"Because I love her. I don't need any other reason! Love cannot be measured by or put into words!"

Shizuo glared back at him, deep in thought. Seiji held his arm high, pen still in hand.

"Which is why I use actions! I'm here to protect her, and that's all there is!"

He thrust the pen downward toward Shizuo's face. The older man easily stopped the pen with his other hand. His eyes were red with rage, and a devilish smile split his face.

"I like you more than Izaya, at least."

Shizuo ripped the pen away from Seiji's hand and held the boy out at arm's length.

"So I'll let you off with this," he said and yanked his arm in so that his head smashed against Seiji's forehead. With a pleasant little crack, Seiji fell to his knees.

Shizuo dropped his victim and made to leave the scene.

"Ugh, these are gonna bleed if I pull them out. Gotta buy some bandages before I extract them. Or maybe instant glue would be better..."

Muttering, Shizuo walked off the street down the alley. The crowd split into two around him, desperately trying to stay out of his path—and one by one, they returned to the mass of pedestrian traffic. Eventually, it was as if nothing had ever happened. Seiji unsteadily climbed to his feet, and the only people watching were doing so out of the corners of their eyes from the distant street corner.

"Damn..." Seiji quietly walked on, his head screaming in agony. "Gotta find her... Gotta help..."

Two police officers approached the stumbling boy.

"Are you all right?"

"Can you walk on your own?"

They had received reports of a fight and came to see, but only Seiji was left, and there were no other traces of the altercation. Shizuo never pulled the pens out of his leg, so whatever blood he lost was all on his pants.

"I'm all right. I just fell, that's all."

"Now, now. We just need you to come to the outpost with us."

"We only want to talk. Besides, you shouldn't be walking in that state."

The policemen appeared to be genuinely concerned for him, but Seiji didn't have time for any of this. He looked around for any signs of her—then heard the growl of that black motorcycle.

He shot around in the right direction, then saw the Black Rider racing for the entrance to the subway...chasing after the girl in pajamas.

"Yama, that's the bike!"

"Forget it, that's above our pay grade. Let Traffic handle it."

Seiji heard none of that. He only had eyes for the girl.

She disappeared into the underground entrance, pulled by someone else. In fact, it looked like—

"Mikado...Ryuugamine," Seiji muttered, recognizing his class rep. He started off for the station.

"Hey, wait!"

"You're gonna hurt yourself!"

The police held him down, and Seiji struggled helplessly. At top condition, he might have been able to momentarily break free, but the damage caused by Shizuo prevented him from using his full strength.

"Let go! Let go of me! She's there! Right there! Let go, let go, let go! Why, dammit, why?! Why is every damn person in the world trying to ruin my love life?! What did I do to deserve this?! What did she do to deserve this?! Let go, let go, let gooooo!"

♂♀

"So your head was walking around, attached to a different body, and just when you thought you had her, a student interfered, and when you pursued the girl, a different student stepped in and took your head away—and you want me to believe that nonsense?"

Shinra spread his arms theatrically in the middle of his apartment, wearing his usual white lab coat. Celty paid his gestures no mind, her fingers limply sliding over the keyboard.

"I'm not demanding that you believe me."

"Oh, but I do. You've never lied to me."

Shinra put on a rousing speech from the other room, hoping to cheer Celty up.

"They say a man's best friends are honesty, sincerity, and wisdom, but in my case, you're the only one I need! Honest, sincere, and wise: I'm proud to have such a perfect life partner!"

"Who said we were life partners?" Celty typed back, but nothing in her reaction suggested disgust at Shinra.

"We could change those three qualities to effort, friendship, and victory instead. How about that?"

"Listen to me. No, not listen—I mean, read the words on the screen," she typed, exasperated. The doctor continued talking, paying her no attention.

"Then I must do my best to live up to them, sparing no effort or expense in traversing my game of fate with you to victory."

"What about friendship?"

"You always have to start as friends, don't you?"

Celty couldn't be bothered to get seriously angry at Shinra's nonsense. She shrugged and decided to take a look at tomorrow's schedule.

"At any rate, I can't sit around feeling sorry for myself. It's possible

that I could finally retrieve my head. I'm pretty sure those uniforms were from Raira, so I'll stake out the school's front gate tomorrow and wait for that student."

Shinra took a look at the unusually long message and cast her a mystified look.

"What comes after that?"

"Isn't it obvious? I'll demand to know the location of my head."

"And then? What will you do?"

"Well," Celty typed, then stopped when she realized what Shinra was getting at.

"This head has its own body now and could only scream when it saw you. What are you going to do with it?"

Her hands lay flat on the keyboard. She had no answer.

"It's living its own life with its own body and apparently knows teenagers well enough to escape with one. What would you do with it? Cut it off the body for your own sake? That's a pretty cruel and vicious thing to do."

After a heavy silence, Celty realized that she was trembling. Shinra spoke the truth. The head did not seem to recognize her. Perhaps it was just the unfamiliar riding suit—but the fact remained that the head had developed its own sense of self that was apart from her.

If I'm going to recover my head for good, it will need to be separated from that body. But is it right to sever a living head from a living body? Could I convince the head to simply stay close to me with its new body? I might be getting it back, but that doesn't address the fundamental issue. Plus, I don't feel like I'm aging at all, but what about my head? Will it still be that young decades later? What if it didn't age while it was isolated, but something changes once both parts of me are back together?

Before she could come to a conclusion, Celty decided to present her basic doubts to Shinra.

"Why does my head have a body that isn't mine anyway?"

"Well, I didn't see it for myself, so nothing I say can be taken as fact. But if you don't mind completely baseless speculation, I can tell you my guess."

Shinra paused for a moment, then delivered his ghastly theory in a matter-of-fact tone.

"They probably found a girl with a fitting body and simply replaced her head with yours."

Celty had imagined that possibility, but it was horrifying to hear stated so bluntly. She was left without a response, so Shinra added further speculation.

"Let's say that a country—or even better, a secret military agency—got its sinister hands on the head in the hopes of creating a legion of undead soldiers. They cloned a fresh new body from the head's cells, then replaced the clone's head with the real one in the hopes of unlocking the dullahan memories hidden within. What do you think?"

"Sounds like a surefire Razzie winner to me," Celty wrote, comparing his idea to the infamous awards for worst movies of the year. Half of her completely disregarded his idea—but the other half thought a secret lab was quite possible.

"Okay, the cloning angle might be a stretch, but it's possible that they could have sewed it onto a corpse. Either that or they kidnapped a living human, then put the head on right after killing it to see if that would bring it back to life. Logically, it's an absolutely absurd idea, but logic also says that you and your head are impossible to begin with. Maybe it *could* take over a dead body."

"This makes me sick. I can't imagine anyone would go that far."

"True, it's not the kind of thing a sane person would do. But people will do just about anything under the right circumstances. Perhaps our mystery person lost a daughter whom he or she wished to keep alive in perpetuity. Or maybe they wanted to *conceal an accidental murder victim by using the body for research.*"

In a way, that idea was even more gruesome than the human experimentation he joked about earlier. Celty typed in a new message, simply to stop him from saying any more.

"Anyway, I want to speak with my head once more. We can talk more after tha—"

Shinra cut her off before she could finish. "And that's how you're going to delay coming to an actual conclusion?"

His voice was deadly serious; there was no trace of the tickled, playful air from just moments earlier.

I know. I get it. Now that I've found my head in this state, I just have to give up.

She let that resignation sink in for a moment, then reluctantly typed, *"I just don't want to admit that everything I've done over the last twenty years has been for nothing."*

She stared sadly at the string of text. Shinra, who had been talking to her from the other side of the apartment, finally came over to Celty's room. He sat down next to her and looked directly at her screen.

"It wasn't for nothing. The last twenty years of your life haven't been for nothing. Nothing you've done is a waste as long as you make use of it in your life ahead."

"And how will I make use of that?"

"Well, for example…if you marry me, you can simply consider the last twenty years the cornerstone of our marital bliss."

Celty had no instant response to his shameless nonsense. Normally she'd ignore it as a joke, but it seemed like Shinra took this topic rather seriously of late.

"May I ask something?"

"Please do."

She wasn't sure if it was right to just ask her question straight out, but after a few moments, Celty summoned her courage and tapped away at the keyboard.

"Do you really love me, Shinra?"

Shinra read the sentence and gaped up at the ceiling in disbelief.

"Why would you ask that *now*?! Ahh, there is a reason that terrible pain in the chest brings tears to one's eyes! What is my sorrow? The fact that you have not believed everything I've done and said to you! My sorrow is that my love for you does not reach your heart!"

"I don't have a head."

"But I'm in love with what's inside! There's more to a human being than looks, remember?"

"I'm not human."

In the end, I'm not a human being. I'm a monster in the shape of a human. The problem is that with my memories trapped in my head, I don't actually know what I am or why I was born and why I exist.

Complex sentiments and unrelatable thoughts. Countless fragments swirled through Celty's heart, but the only thing she could impart were simple words on a computer screen.

"Aren't you frightened of holding affection for something inhuman? How can you say these things to a being that doesn't even follow the same basic laws of physics?"

The letters sped up across the screen. In response, Shinra's voice grew harder and stronger. He sounded exasperated.

"I can't believe you're asking me that after twenty years together... Why would you even think about this? We share a mutual understanding—if we love each other, what's the problem? If you decide that you hate me, I guess that's that... But we're not just forced to live together out of cold mutual dependence, are we? Can't you have some trust in me?"

It was rare for Shinra to sincerely plead his own case, but the abundance of ten-dollar words said that he was not yet at the end of his rope.

"I do trust you. If there's anyone I don't trust, it's myself."

She decided to reveal some of her own insecurity while he was still feeling in control.

"I have no self-confidence. Even if I was in love with you or some other human being, would our romantic values actually be the same? Yes, I probably do love you. I just don't know if it's what a human would call romantic love."

"That's something every human being goes through in their youth. It's not as if every human being shares the same views and values. Love to me may not be the same as love to the great writer Osamu Dazai. In fact, it's probably different... At any rate, I can say that I love you, and you just said that you love me, so where's the problem?"

He sounded like a teacher explaining something to a student. The dullahan's fingers stopped moving.

"Yesterday I said I wanted to understand your values as a dullahan—but whatever your answer is, it won't change the fact that I love you," Shinra said in a voice free of shyness or hesitation. His expression was completely serious. Celty thought this over for a moment, choosing her words carefully.

"Give me some time to think."

"I'll wait as long as it takes," Shinra replied, his smile serene. Celty had to ask one other thing.

"Is it really me you want? There are so many human women out there, why would you choose a headle...a nonhuman woman? Why?"

"Ha-ha. There's no accounting for taste, right?"

"You're one to talk. And don't make it sound like you have to be a weirdo to like me."

Even as she typed back her snappy response, Celty felt something hot swirling in her chest. She knew that it was her feeling for Shinra.

If I had a heart, I'd hear it pounding away in my ears.

But that thought, that contradiction, plagued Celty even more. It only underscored the great differences between her and Shinra.

Dullahans had no hearts. According to Shinra's father after he dissected her, she was constructed much like a human being—but the organs were all for show and did not actually function. There were veins, but no blood running through them. Without any red blood, her meat was the color of pure flesh, like a model of a human body. He didn't know how her body worked and moved. He didn't know what she used for a source of energy. And despite that, any wounds she suffered healed at incredible speed.

After the dissection, Shinra's father asked her, "How do you actually die?"

Ten years later, Shinra said, "You must be a shadow. You're just the shadow of your head or an actual body in some other world. The source of your energy to move means nothing to your shadow."

It was nonsense to think of a shadow moving of its own will, but then again, nothing about her existence made sense, so she followed Shinra's advice and stopped thinking about it. She needed to spend the next few days focusing on her head. And depending on the results of that period, she would make a decision about her life.

Celty clenched a fist and pictured the faces of the two students she saw today.

They both looked serious. The first one glared back fiercely, without a hint of fear toward Celty or Shizuo. The other one showed obvious signs of fright at Celty, but he still had a *smile* on his face when he looked at her. It was the expression of one looking at a demon or monster worthy of fear and respect.

She then thought about herself.

But perhaps that's all just my own selfish interpretation.

She took her interpretation of the others' feelings from their expressions, including the eyes, but she couldn't be certain that it was true. She did not have her own eyes or face with which to express delight, anger or sadness. She didn't have a brain to process human emotions.

She didn't even know where her thoughts or feelings were coming from. How could she accurately sense the emotions of others?

Angry eyes, sad eyes, human morals—these were all pieces of knowledge she had picked up in this city. TV shows, comics, movies—Shinra's tastes biased her selection of these things, but her actual experiences in town and news reports helped to balance that out. The problem was that all these things were just information gleaned from elsewhere. She wouldn't know if they were *true* or not unless she was a human being herself.

That was why she was always plagued by the insecurity she revealed to Shinra earlier. She didn't know if she truly had emotions. It was a thought that constantly troubled her.

In the past, she didn't care about these things. She was too busy seeking her head. But in the last few years, as the Internet gave her increased opportunities to contact people, she couldn't help but wonder how close her feelings and values were to those of humans.

At first, she found it frightening and needed Shinra's help, but now Celty was at the computer at virtually all times when not working or searching for her head. Once she got a model with a built-in DVD drive and TV tuner, she could get her movies and TV shows there, which only increased the time she spent before the computer.

Celty increased her contact with others over the Internet. People separated by their PCs did not know each other's faces or pasts. Which was fine with her, because she didn't even have a face. And yet, the connections were real. In real life, she only knew a few people through Shinra, and only he and his father knew exactly what she was. Rumors had spread about the headless rider, but the rumors didn't identify her as a woman or a dullahan.

She didn't feel a particular need to hide these things, but neither did she plan to reveal them.

Even after what Shinra said, I still want to have human values. If the persona that I own now is "human," I don't want to lose that.

Celty was not a human being. But she still felt anxiety. If she got back her head but the memories did not return, what should she do? What kind of face would a human make in this situation?

Her knowledge contained the answer, but she herself could not say what it was.

Chapter 10

Dollars, Opening

In the meeting room of Lab Six, seated on a chair in the corner, Seiji grumbled to himself, head downcast. His sister Namie gently embraced him in an attempt to ease his discomfort.

"Everything's fine, Seiji. Leave this to us. We're going to get her back. Don't worry about a thing."

The police dragged Seiji to their box station after Shizuo knocked him out, but without a victim to finger him or even a firm consensus on who *was* the victim, he was released without any charges or punishment.

Maybe it was my sister pulling strings. She did arrive to pick me up extremely fast, Seiji thought. It didn't actually bother him. *I know she's in love with me in some kind of sick way. It only comes out of a weird possessiveness. But I don't mind. No matter who else loves me, it won't change my own choice. I live for my own love and nothing else.*

And if I have to stomp all over the love others give me in order to do that, so be it. I'm sure she'd be happy knowing she served as a stepping-stone for the sake of her beloved.

Meanwhile, Namie could read Seiji like a book. But she didn't mind. As long as that head was in her possession, Seiji needed her. That head, the very target of her darkest jealousy, was the key to the equation. Namie grinned in self-mockery at the irony of it all.

The sight of her shamelessly doting on her brother put a kind of fear in the minds of everyone who witnessed the scene.

One of her employees overcame his consternation and called out for her attention.

"You don't need to worry about a thing, Seiji. Leave everything to us." And with that, his sister quietly left the room.

"Do we have details?"

"We've got the address of this Ryuugamine that Mr. Seiji spoke of. It's a run-down apartment building right next to Ikebukuro Station."

Namie was receiving the report from her subordinates slightly down the hallway from the meeting room. The fact that the employee was giving Seiji that title spoke to the strength of the Yagiri family within the company.

Unlike her warm, loving manner in the meeting room, Namie was as cold as ice as she gave the orders.

"Then gather up the underlings and retrieve the target."

"That's a conspicuous place for a daylight operation—"

"I don't care," she stated flatly, brooking no further discussion.

If we wait for nightfall, my brother's going to run off and try to find this Ryuugamine on his own.

Namie cared more about Seiji's safety than the danger of the situation. But she was professional enough not to show the tiniest ounce of this priority when Seiji wasn't around. She was all business.

"Inform all of our available muscle at once. I don't care who's there or if they're taken dead or alive. Depending on the circumstances, I may want you to dispose of them on the spot."

There wasn't a shred of humanity in her eyes. The other men felt cold sweat trickle down their backs.

♂♀

Today was the start of normal classes for Raira Academy. But even then, it mostly consisted of teacher introductions and guidance on the course of the entire school year, and the only classes with real lectures were math and world history.

Nothing else noteworthy or problematic occurred. The first day passed by.

If anything weighed on Mikado's mind, it was the absence of not only Mika Harima, but now Seiji Yagiri, the Health Committee representative. After Anri had explained what happened between the two of them the day before, it was hard not to feel a connection in their absences. An uneasy murmur rose in his chest.

On top of that, there was also his unease over the girl with amnesia back at his house.

She did not remember anything more after waking up this morning and refused to go to the hospital or police. The suggestion of the hospital, in particular, brought a look of terror into her eyes.

"Oh...I'll be fine! I'll just stay here and wait for you!" she said, looking far calmer today than she had the day before. In fact, she looked quite secure and focused for someone suffering memory loss.

That at least gave Mikado enough confidence to leave her behind while he was at school, but he still had no idea what to do with her after that. Without knowing her identity, there was no getting around the fact that she'd need to be handed over to the police at some point. He thought about the option of Masaomi's house, but Masaomi commuted to school from his family's home.

Mikado spent the entire day mulling over what to do, and before he arrived at an answer, the day was done. There was a brief introductory meeting for all of the class reps, after which he headed outside with Anri, hoping to ask for any updates on Mika Harima.

"Have you heard from her?" Mikado didn't have anything else to talk about and felt awkward not saying anything, so he decided to be direct.

"Actually, I haven't heard a thing from her since yesterday afternoon..."

"Oh, I see..."

He shouldn't have asked. Now he was even more worried about the fact that Seiji was absent as well. He began to wonder about the possibility of some kind of murder-suicide but didn't dare say that out loud to Anri.

Masaomi's presence would have helped out a lot, but from what he heard, the Discipline Committee was still busy with introductions. Apparently, Masaomi and the representative from Mikado's class had launched into an argument that no one else was quite able to stop.

He decided his best action was just to go home for today and was preparing to say good-bye to Anri at the ornate Western-style front gate when someone shouted at them from the side.

"Aha! That's him, Takashi, right there!"

A girl was pointing in Mikado and Anri's direction. It was the one whose cell phone had been stomped by Izaya yesterday, and she was escorted by a burly looking guy.

Before he could even register a sense of dread at the unfolding situation, Mikado was lifted up by the collar.

"I hear you know the guy who busted my girl's cell."

"I don't *know him* know him—"

You should be telling the police about this, not your boyfriend, Mikado wanted to yell at Bully A next to the guy, but he couldn't speak with a hand pulling him up by the collar.

"So where's this dick you were standin' around with?"

Straight as an arrow—he asked about Izaya directly, without allowing Mikado any say.

Elusive as quicksilver—a pitch-black bike silently appeared behind the man.

Swift as the wind—still on the bike, a humanoid shadow kicked Takashi to the ground.

Survival of the fittest—out of nowhere, Izaya Orihara landed on the fallen man's back with both feet.

Man's inhumanity to man—Izaya jumped up and down on his back repeatedly.

Like greased lightning—this happened before Mikado's eyes in the span of ten seconds.

"Thank you."

Izaya bowed ostentatiously in the direction of the shocked Anri, her bully, and all the other students who happened to be passing by. He was still standing atop the unconscious Takashi.

"You knew that hitting girls wasn't my thing, so you made sure to prepare a guy for me instead! Now that's the sign of a dedicated woman. I'd love to make you my girlfriend, but sorry. You're just not my type. Get lost."

It was all very cruel, but the girl was off and running before he even finished speaking. She didn't even spare a backward glance at Takashi underneath Izaya's feet. Mikado had to admit that he felt a bit sorry for the guy.

The girl's face already vanishing from his memory, Izaya turned to Mikado.

"Heya, it's too bad we were interrupted yesterday. I don't think we have to worry about our friend Shizu butting in here. I thought it would be rude to look up your address and barge in, so I decided to lie in wait at the school entrance instead," he said, smiling all the while. Mikado didn't know why Izaya was smiling or what reason he would have to seek him out. But that actually wasn't true—he knew of one possible reason. Mikado couldn't openly acknowledge it, though. He clenched a fist.

Seemingly unaware of the boy's train of thought, Izaya tilted his head in confusion.

"By the way, what's the Black Rider doing here?"

I could ask the same of you, Celty thought to herself.

She had indeed found the student who escorted her head away yesterday. She intervened to save him from being pounded, but Izaya's presence was a mystery to her.

Celty couldn't imagine Izaya getting involved with an ordinary person, much less a teenage student. Was he the son of some powerful politician? Or some kind of despicable pusher, spreading drugs to children in elementary and middle school?

But whoever the boy was made no difference to Celty now.

All that mattered was whether he knew the location of her head or not.

Mikado snapped to his senses with a shock when he realized that Anri was even more dazed by the incident than he was.

"W-well, Sonohara, I should really be going!"

"Huh…? Um, okay…"

And with that awkward farewell, Mikado quickly left the scene. As he suspected, the shadow and villain followed him. Once a safe distance away from the school, he timidly turned back and decided that Izaya was more likely to understand him.

"Umm... I don't know what's going on here... But if you'd like, we can go back to my..."

Mikado stopped and held his breath. If he took them back to his house, the Black Rider would find that girl. In fact, she was probably the only reason that the Black Rider had come for him in the first place.

"Uh...well, actually, there's something I'd like to ask the rider in black..."

Celty pulled a PDA out of the shadow riding suit and typed, "What is it?"

So there was a way for them to communicate after all. Mikado was slightly relieved but also noted that the situation was taking a turn into even more surreal waters.

I feel like crying.

♂♀

Just a few minutes away from the station by foot was a building. It was hard to guess exactly how old it was, but the countless tiny cracks in the walls and the abundant ivy said enough on their own.

Once the building came into view, Mikado stopped and said, "Well, my apartment is on the first floor of this building...but I want an explanation first. Who in the world are you people?"

Celty avoided mentioning anything about her head or her true identity. She only typed, "I recently ran into a girl I knew who had gone missing, but she fled for some reason I cannot fathom."

But Mikado was not naive enough to take such a transparent excuse at face value. Celty decided that she didn't have a choice but to give him the truth.

She asked Izaya to give them some momentary privacy, then took Mikado around the back of the building. Summoning her courage, she started typing on the PDA.

"How much do you know about me?"

Mikado stared at the tiny LCD screen, then gave the question some thought.

"Well...you're sort of an urban legend, and you ride a motorcycle without headlights that makes no sound. And..."

He paused, sucking in a deep breath, then letting it all out at once. Along with the fear in his voice, there was something expectant, even excited.

"...you don't have a head."

Celty typed, *"And do you believe all of it?"*

She showed him the screen, then immediately regretted it. What human being would possibly believe that? But Mikado nodded.

Huh?

She couldn't hide her shock. Mikado went on.

"Um...can you show me what's inside your helmet?"

Celty stared him right in the face.

Aha, just like yesterday.

That strange expression again, a mix of fear, expectation, despair, and joy all in one. And the student with all of these emotions in his eyes wanted her to expose her true face to him. Celty hesitated, then typed in her PDA.

"Do you swear you won't scream?"

She knew it was a stupid question, but she had to be sure. Celty hadn't removed her helmet for anyone in the last twenty years but Shinra. There had been a few times it popped off in the middle of a fight, but the only reaction she got from the witnesses was a grimace of terror.

But this young man named Mikado was facing his fear directly. He believed that her word was not a lie or a joke and still asked her to see. It was foolish to ask such a man if he wouldn't scream.

Mikado's reaction was exactly as she expected. His head nodded vigorously, and at the same time, Celty pushed the visor of the full helmet upward.

Darkness. There was nothing before his eyes but empty space. Technically, it wasn't *empty* in the vacuum sense, but that made no difference to Mikado. It was a space where what should exist did not, and the presence or absence of anything to fill that space was immaterial.

Nothing. There's nothing there. It's not a magic trick—but if it were, I'd sure like to know how to pull it off.

For the first instant, Mikado's eyes were wide with terror, but it did not lead to a scream. He stifled that emotion, and his shock turned to elation. There were even little tears forming at the bottom of his eyes.

"Thank you...thank you."

What he was thanking her for was unclear, but his eyes were full of childlike wonder. She was completely at a loss for what to do.

It was rare enough for her to be thanked, much less meet acceptance for the idea that she had no head, that the situation was entirely baffling—but not in a bad or uncomfortable way.

After Celty explained the situation to him, Mikado happily agreed to let her see the "head girl." When he told the dullahan that the girl's memory was gone, Celty had no immediate answer. She said she had to see the girl so that the misunderstanding could be corrected.

They called Izaya back at this point, but he claimed that his business could wait until later. He stayed back and watched the other two.

"All right... Please wait here for now. I'll go in first and talk to her. I don't want her to see you first before I can explain your presence here, in case she gets the wrong idea."

"I understand."

Izaya piped up with a sarcastic-sounding "Very cautious—that's a good stance to take."

They waited outside the apartment building as Mikado went in. As they stood there, Izaya said, "By the way, courier, I hadn't caught your name before this. Didn't realize you weren't from around these parts."

He grinned. Based on the smirk, he probably already knew that, and it was meant to be a dig at Celty's uptight refusal to name herself. She understood all of this already and chose to ignore him. It was possible that he even knew *what* she was—but only cobbled together from eyewitness accounts, not because he recognized her as a fairy.

Not to mention that any levelheaded person would not even imagine that the Black Rider could be anything but a human being. The problem was that Izaya was not levelheaded. He was not a man to be underestimated.

"So what's taking him so long?"

It had been more than five minutes. Even if he had failed in his negotiation, he should have at least come back out to explain by now.

"Maybe I should take a look."

The apartment building was too quiet. Celty felt a creeping unease steal over her. That unease was amplified by a cleaning service van parked next to the building.

A professional cleaner at a dump like this? Not likely...

Her fear was well-founded.

"I'll ask again... We know you were keeping a girl here in your apartment. We just wanna know where she is now."

"There's no use denying it. We found a woman's hair in your bed. Pretty short cut but clearly longer than yours."

Two men were waiting for Mikado when he entered his apartment. They were wearing work uniforms, but one look at their faces said they weren't simple laborers. Mikado was shoved to the floor before he could say a word, and they kept interrogating him, over and over, in low, menacing voices.

They were looking for the "head girl," but Mikado wanted to know her location just as much as they did. Either someone else had already taken her away, or she'd gotten up and run off on her own...

"I-I don't know! Please, I really don't know!"

"Listen, kid. You've seen our faces. We could make you disappear right now," one said like some kind of gloating movie villain. Mikado felt tears of fright welling up in his eyes. He felt so stupid—just moments ago, he'd been filled with joy at the sight of something inhuman and alien, and now he was mired in terror of plain old humanity again. He lamented his carelessness.

"Someone's here!"

The men jumped up without hesitation and raced out. In a few moments, the van's engine started outside.

"Whew...I'm saved..."

In particular, he was saved from the shame of shedding tears of fright. He did not, however, avoid tears of relief.

Celty raced past the door of the apartment and made to chase after the van, but Izaya said there was no need to do that.

"I'm pretty sure they're from Yagiri Pharmaceuticals. I recognize the van," he noted, a free piece of intel from the info broker.

"Yagiri...Pharmaceuticals...?"

"Yep. A company down on its luck, in danger of being bought out by foreign capital."

When he processed that name, Mikado's teary eyes went wide. Yes, it was the same name as his classmate—but he recognized that name from *something else.*

The tears drained back into their ducts.

A girl bearing a head gone missing. A dullahan. Yagiri. Pharmaceutical company. Missing people. Mika Harima. Anri Sonohara's story. Seiji Yagiri. Kidnappers. Dollars.

Various fragments of information floated into Mikado's head and disappeared. The free flow of concepts coalesced into a theory.

In the now-quiet apartment, Mikado quickly started his computer. While he waited for it to boot up, he turned on his phone, which had been off since school, and immediately checked his e-mail.

Celty watched him curiously. In contrast, Izaya was like a hunter watching over rare prey, his sharp eyes gleaming wickedly.

"You know, I had my doubts," the information broker started. Mikado opened his Internet browser the instant his computer had fully booted and typed in some kind of code with tremendous speed. He was logging into a website. After that came the rhythmic sound of mouse clicking.

Mikado examined the page for a little while, then turned to his guests.

Celty shivered despite herself. His eyes did not have the bedraggled look of the boy who'd been helpless to stop the circumstances around him for the past hour. His were the eyes of a hawk following its quarry, endlessly deep and sharp. He bowed to them.

She was taken aback. He didn't seem to be the same weak-willed student who was just here moments ago.

"I need your help. Can I count on your assistance for just a short while?" he asked, full of purpose and determination. "The pawns are in the *palm of my hand.*"

Izaya patted Celty on the shoulder and boasted as though he'd just found a new toy. "Jackpot."

Celty looked back and forth between the two, unsure of what Izaya meant. She didn't know what had just happened, but she could tell that

Izaya was more excited now than she'd ever seen before. And even more excited was Mikado Ryuugamine.

His face still had the trappings of childhood, and now his eyes were shining like a boy who'd just received a new toy. There was no sign of the tears of terror anymore, only an expression of strong will and elation that said he was in full control of himself.

Over the last few days since his arrival in Ikebukuro, Mikado had run across a number of baffling, inexplicable events. And right before his eyes, they were all connecting into one convoluted case.

He breathed heavily, mentally examining each piece of the puzzle to make sure they fit together.

Boring days. Familiar sights. Stuck in place with no future.

It was to escape all of these things that he decided to move to Ikebukuro. And now he could feel himself achieving that escape at last.

Mikado Ryuugamine realized that he was becoming a kind of lead player in this story. At the same time, an enemy had appeared that threatened his new life—and his life, period.

In his state of excitement, he felt no hesitation or fear toward the need to eliminate that foe.

The time had come to speak. He started to explain everything about himself to Celty and Izaya.

♂♀

In the hallway outside of Lab Six beneath Yagiri Pharmaceuticals, a cold voice split the air.

"What do you mean…she wasn't there?"

"Apparently, when the underlings reached the place, there were signs that the lock had already been pried open…and no sign of the girl inside."

"So someone got the jump on us?"

"The place is a dump, so it's unlikely to be a burglar."

Namie's brows knitted together in thought. If the student took her out, then what would be the purpose of breaking open the lock? On the other hand, she couldn't think of anyone aside from her company who would want the girl.

"And the student who lives there?"

"When they returned to report, they claimed they were prepared to bring him back with them, but he had…company."

"So why didn't they bring him, company and all? Such incompetence…"

She clicked her tongue in irritation just before her phone started ringing. The display said it was an unlisted number, but she answered anyway on the chance that it was important.

"Hello?"

"Um, is this Miss Namie Yagiri?"

The voice was young. It sounded like a teenage boy, probably in middle school.

"Yes. Who is this?"

"My name is Mikado Ryuugamine."

"—!"

Namie's heart silently upped its pulse. Her brother's classmate, the one who took the girl away with him. There was an eeriness to the fact that he was calling right as they'd been talking about him. She wondered how he'd even gotten her number.

Meanwhile, the voice on the other end of the call continued on its business.

"As it happens, we have a certain young lady under our care at this moment…"

After a brief pause, the phone produced a message that made no sense at all, devoid of even the slightest bit of tension, as matter-of-fact as if it were asking her out to dinner.

"…How about we make a deal?"

♂♀

11:00 p.m., the same day, Ikebukuro

Night had fallen on 60-Kai Street in Ikebukuro. The shutters were down on virtually every business except for the bars, and unlike during the day, the pedestrians no longer ruled the street—there were actual cars going to and fro now.

A young man in a bartender's uniform leaning against a streetlamp spoke to an enormous black man.

"What is life? What do people live for? Someone asked me that once, and I beat him within an inch of his life. It'd be one thing if it was a starry-eyed dreamer of a teenage girl, but from a grown man who wanted to be a yakuza but tried to get out because he didn't like running errands? It's practically a crime."

"That's right!"

"Everyone's free to think what they want about their own life. No one can deny you that. But why the hell would you ask for answers from another person? So I told him, 'This is your life, live so you can die,' while his pupils dilated. Then again, that was the bar manager, so I probably screwed up again."

"That's right!"

"...Simon, I get the feeling you don't understand what I'm saying."

"That's right!"

Shizuo Heiwajima bellowed and threw a nearby bicycle at Simon, who caught it one-handed. The town swallowed up this scene, assimilating it—business as usual.

When night hit Ikebukuro, it was a completely different place than during the daytime. It was just as crowded and chaotic, but blackness swallowed everything, so that the world seemed to be in negative. Nowadays, more people were utilizing cheap manga cafés to spend the night than more expensive hotels. Missing the last train was no longer the big deal it had once been.

On streets close to the train station, karaoke barkers hustled about, latching onto groups of students and new employees out for a celebration. Most of those groups already had their next destinations picked out, and they gradually faded away from the street.

People left drinking establishments and headed home, young people partied through the night, and smatterings of foreigners dotted the scene. It wasn't on the same level as when the sun was out, but the night had its own crowded bustle.

However...

In front of the Tokyu Hands store that intersected the main road, two people stood apart from the crowd.

One was a student wearing his uniform jacket. The other was a grown woman wearing a business suit.

Now that they were both at the agreed-upon location, Namie Yagiri asked the boy, "You're Mikado? You're so mature—not at all the child I was expecting. Or is it the polite ones who are most dangerous these days?"

Her voice was soft but rimmed with infinite frost.

They did not leave for another location to talk, but stayed in place right outside the building. The chilly, overbearing air she wielded kept all of the karaoke and host clubs' solicitors away, as well as any overeager men looking for companionship.

Meanwhile, Mikado wore his Raira Academy blazer, but no attitude that made him anything but a normal student. The solicitors weren't going to bother upselling a lone teenager like him. In fact, it was more likely that if he hung around in his current outfit, he'd draw the attention of the police for being where he shouldn't.

They were two souls who didn't fit in the scene for opposite reasons. A quiet tension fomented between them.

"So…what is your proposition?" Namie asked.

He'd managed to get her to negotiate in person; he probably knew just about everything. The girl must have told him all that she knew over the course of the evening.

"It's simple. As I told you over the phone, I have the person you're looking for."

This did not unnerve Namie. If he was proposing this deal in possession of all of the facts, he really had to be a child. It was the height of folly.

He must have designated this location right in the middle of 60-Kai Street thinking that such a public location meant they couldn't play rough with him. But of course, she had not come alone. The company's security team, normally in charge of guarding the research lab, was disguised in the crowd as ordinary salarymen. Nearly a dozen loyal employees were on standby with stun batons. Just in case they were necessary, vans parked along 60-Kai Street and in side alleys contained more underlings and other hired muscle types, about twenty in total.

It wasn't just the one boy, of course. He wouldn't be trying to strike such a deal without others on his side. Hence the necessity of such a large force behind her.

In addition, Namie had brought a reasonable amount of cash to help strike a deal, in recognition of his admirable pluck. As long as she got the girl back, they could crush the boy in an instant if he thought he could open his mouth.

"How much do you want?" she asked directly. No need for theatrics in such a silly transaction. There was no telling where he might have hidden a recorder, if she was careless and gave away some kind of personal secret.

But his answer caught her by surprise.

"It's not money, actually."

"What are you dealing for, then?"

"Don't you know? The truth."

What does he mean? she wondered, baffled.

Mikado laid out his conclusion. "Let's start with an admission of what your brother—Seiji Yagiri—is responsible for doing."

"_____!"

The warm spring air instantly turned to midwinter chill. After a long silence, Namie fixed him with a stare that froze anyone who looked at it and spoke in a voice that demolished any who heard it.

"What...did you...just say?"

"Confess what your brother did to Mika Harima—and what you did to her body after that. Unfortunately, since there's only circumstantial evidence, I'll need you to turn yourselves in."

Despite the easiness of his speech, sweat flooded Mikado's palms. Black rage was exploding off of her. If he let his guard down just the tiniest bit, he might burst into tears.

"I think that course of action would do the least damage to your company."

"Oh, dear... Yes, I see... You don't want money at all. You just want our lab to be shut down for good..."

"In order to guarantee her freedom—not to mention my safety, since she ended up at my home—that seems to be the only option. If you simply bow out, I don't see why that should lead to the downfall of the company."

As he spoke, Mikado noticed that her reaction had started to go strange.

"Oh...oh...such a shame... You see, the company means absolutely nothing to me."

She pierced Mikado with a look that he couldn't distinguish between laughing or crying. He grappled with this new revelation, waiting for her next line. All of Mikado's hair stood on end as he fought against the pressure of receiving his death sentence.

She didn't even seem to be the same coolheaded woman who arrived in front of the department store building—but her voice was still soft and calm.

"You can crush my company, bomb it to hell, burn it to the ground, and I wouldn't care a whit. But...the one thing I won't stand for...is someone who tries to *stand between my brother and what he wants.*"

Her answer was simple. So simple, in fact, that Mikado's eyes narrowed in a kind of relief.

Oh, I get it. She's one of those *people. No wonder she's been doing things that go above and beyond her company's bottom line.*

At the same moment that her fists clenched, Mikado tightened his own grip on the cell phone in his pocket, pressing the button to send an e-mail.

This would explain it.

He was nearly bowled over backward by her incredible fixation on her brother but held his ground and glared back at her.

One person's already been killed, the body was used to create a totally new person, and now she's trying to have me killed, too. I think the last part is what makes me angriest. I care about myself most of all. I would do anything for my own sake. That's what makes people like her, who replace the "my" in "my sake" with another person, so aggravating. And someone who would use that excuse to ruin the lives of others is especially, especially, especially unforgivable!

Anger began to bubble up within Mikado. He was obsessed with all things extraordinary and abnormal but being the victim of irrational, unfair circumstances was something else entirely. He launched into Namie.

"I've never heard such an awful thing. You're going to make Yagiri miserable for your own twisted, selfish reasons."

"What do you mean? If you're going to brave the depths of the underworld at your age, and all you can come up with is that clichéd garbage...then shut that impertinent mouth of yours right now!" she roared like some kind of witch's curse, closing a step toward Mikado.

But he did not pull back.

"You're right, I only know how to speak in clichés. But what's wrong with that? And which one of us is incapable of comprehending the obvious fact that there's a price to be paid for taking a human life?"

Mikado took a step of his own, returning her glare.

"You've watched too much TV. The old-fashioned kind with a moral at the end of the story! Do you know where we are?! This is the real world! You're not on TV, you're not in a magazine, and you're not a hero. Learn your place, boy!"

They each approached another step. Namie's voice was overflowing with cold fury, but those words on their own were not enough to stop him. He'd suffered the nonsense of Masaomi Kida's conversations every day. Compared to them, her arguments were at least logical, and thus easy to rebut.

"That's right. I want to see what's clean and unsoiled. I want things to act in harmony. All those clichés and predictable outcomes are familiar and beloved to me. But what's wrong with that? What's wrong with wishing for that to happen in real life? It's because of the nature of reality that we desire them! I'm not going to claim it's for the sake of others; I want them because I enjoy seeing that! Yes, it's a common cliché. And the fact that it's such a cliché just shows you how much everyone thinks about it!"

He tried to overwhelm her with statements and questions, some of which he didn't even believe in himself. But he wasn't just trying to provoke her out of desperation—he was trying to keep her attention *focused on himself* for as long as he could.

When he felt the moment was right, Mikado tensed the finger waiting on his phone button.

Once I press this button, there's no going back. I'll be entering a place one should never go. I wanted to avoid this if possible, but based on her reaction, I don't have another choice. I don't have the strength or intelligence to challenge someone who doesn't respond to logic. And I don't have the time to try, because I've got to find a way to survive this situation first.

Mikado sucked in a deep breath of determination and pushed the switch as he let it out.

So my only choice—is to rely on numbers!

"This is ridiculous. Enough discussion," Namie said, then slowly raised her hand. "I don't care how many friends you have. We can come up with plenty of truth serum."

Her face glowed with a radiant smile as her hand stretched overhead. She never realized that there could be such pleasure in eliminating her brother's enemies.

Some of Namie's subordinates saw her hand rise.

"That's the signal. Just grab the kid."

"Hey...hang on, what if he's working with the cops? We could be screwing ourselves..."

"At this point, who cares? She certainly ain't seein' the big picture. Bring on the cops—once the dust has settled, the broad will handle everything."

The more gung ho of the men ignored his hesitant partner, dropped his drunken salaryman act, and did a brief scan of the area.

"Huh...?"

He noticed something and checked with his partner. "It's like... eleven o'clock, right?"

"Yeah."

He felt a subtle chill creep over him.

"Then...where'd all these people come from?"

Just as the first man burst out of the crowd and smoothly, naturally made his way closer to Mikado—

Beebeebeep, beebeebeep.

It was the sound of a cell phone receiving a text.

At first, the man thought it was his own, but then he realized he didn't have his phone on him. It was just someone else's message tone coming from very close by.

But when he turned in the direction of the sound, he saw a very large black man, towering well over six feet tall. It was the giant well known along this street—Simon. The man averted his gaze and kept walking so as not to make more eye contact.

Then the bleeping beeps were followed by a little song.

He turned in the direction of that sound and saw a bartender wearing sunglasses—Shizuo Heiwajima, the so-called brawling puppet of Ikebukuro. What was he doing there?

He turned in yet another direction and saw several people of an entirely different type, each one busy reading an e-mail off of their phone.

"...?!"

That's when they noticed something. As several different chimes played on, more songs started up, forming an ugly, clashing harmony.

Beebeebeebeep, beebeebeebeep.

More text notifications, at least a dozen from every direction.

"?!"

At last, Namie and her men realized that something strange was happening.

The mixed crowd of countless milling figures had grown into what would more accurately be termed a mob. Even those whose phones hadn't gone off were pulling them out of pockets, drawn by the vibration setting. But the vast majority were beeping and ringing incessantly.

And then...

Too late to do anything about it, the little group was *drowned in waves of ringtones.*

Tone, tone, tone. Melody tone ringtone, ringtone, harmonic tone, harmony.

*tonetonetonetonetonemelodymelodymelodyringringringringtone-
toneharmonicnicnicnicharmony*

*harmonyharmonyharmonytonetonemelotonedytonemelotonetone-
tonemelotoneringtoneringtoneingtonetonehartoneringmeltoneingnic-
tonehartoneritoneingharmingtonemelotoningringmeloharmo*

*tonetonetonetonetonetonetonetonetonetonetonetonetonetone-
tonetonetonetonetonetonetonetonetonetonetonetonetonetone-
tonetonetonetonetonetonetonetonetonetonetonetonetonetone-
tonetonetonetonetonetonetonetonetonetonetonetonetonetone-
tonetonetonetone*

*tone, tonetonetonetone, tonetonetonetonetonetone, tonetonetonetone
tone, tonetonetone tonetone*

tonetonetone, tonetonetonetone, tonetone, tonetone, tonetonetone, tone, tonetone tonetonetone, tone

tonetone, tone, tonetonetoneto, tonetonetonetonetonetone, tonetonetonetone, tonetonetone, tone

tone, tonetone, tone, tone, tonetonetone, tone, tonetonetone, tonetone, tonetone, tonetone, tone, tone

And as the ringtones gradually calmed and faded out, Namie's group found they were the center of attention.

Gazes. They were singled out from the crowd by a sea of gazes.

Dozens, if not hundreds, of people in the surrounding crowd were all turned in their direction, staring—sometimes speaking with the person beside them—casting them into sharp relief, as though they were the players of some kind of theater, performing in a special space cut out of the surroundings...

"What...what is this...? What's happening...? Who the hell are these people?!" Namie screamed. The scene had overturned not just her expectations, but everything she thought was normal.

But the stares did not stop. It was as though they had made enemies out of the entire world.

Lost in the terrible shock of the moment was the fact that the boy she'd been negotiating with had slipped into the crowd, disappearing into the sea of gazes.

The *founder of the Dollars* turned into one of the mob, unbeknownst to anyone.

♂♀

"Whoa, can you believe that? Izaya and Shizuo on the same street, and they're not fighting or anything!" Karisawa bubbled. She was sitting in a van parked on the side of the street.

"That's just because Shizuo hasn't noticed him. Still, this is wild. Is it me, or are there even some students in the mix? Not that hardly any of them are wearing their uniforms at this time of day."

One of the cars parked on 60-Kai Street was the van that Kadota, Yumasaki, and the others drove. Inside, Kadota's friends—and a new girl they just picked up this morning—watched the scene outside with trepidation.

The girl was one they'd kidnapped before she could be *kidnapped*, from a rickety, old apartment building near Ikebukuro Station. By torturing those thugs, the group learned that a Yagiri Pharmaceuticals research lab was behind the event. Just as they were about to finish up with their victims, the leader of the thugs got a text message that appeared to be a code.

After forcing him to decode the message, they learned that it contained an address, with a note that there was a "girl with a scar on her neck" there, and a simple text drawing of a door. There was also an image attached to the e-mail—creepily enough, it was a picture of the girl's severed head. In the image, it almost looked like it was *alive*, but the file labeled it a "re-creation."

Kadota asked the thugs what the door was supposed to mean. They said it was a corruption of D.O.A.—dead or alive. With that in mind, the group decided to swing by the apartment before anyone else arrived, pick the lock, and take the girl to safety.

All the other kidnappers who got the same message must have been stationed outside of Toshima Ward, because Kadota's group was first on the scene in Ikebukuro and succeeded in their mission.

They didn't know who the girl shivering in the back of the van was yet, but Kadota made sure to report it through the form on the Dollars' website. It was designed to reduce conflict between the various members of the Dollars, but it was almost unheard of for members to run into each other on the street.

Even if they did, it was typically no more than the friendly relationship that developed between Karisawa's team and Kaztano, the illegal immigrant. Until this moment, none of them knew that Simon and Shizuo were also members.

The idea of illegal immigrants being on the Net was strange, but it turned out that they were recruited through old-fashioned word of mouth in real life. The Dollars were apparently growing through more mediums than just the Internet.

And that led to today—the group's first-ever meetup.

"Sheesh, how many people is that? Y'know, it looks less like a gang meetup than some kind of flash mob from a major forum or something."

"Well, the Dollars aren't exactly your typical color gang. Hell, the team color is camouflage."

"By the way, what's the leader like?"

"No idea..."

As Yumasaki and Karisawa chattered happily away, Kadota groaned in the driver's seat. "Geez... Is this what the Dollars really are? Damn... What's going on...?"

He was conflicted with equal parts bewilderment at having been part of such an inexplicable group and astonishment at the sheer power of the sight. It was far beyond the scale of any color gang.

♂♀

At a glance, it didn't look like a meetup at all. Each person wore their own outfit and stood where they were without order or reason. They were simply there as they were—on their own or in small groups of like-minded friends.

Some were office workers, some were teenage girls in their high school uniforms, some were exceedingly plain college students, some were foreigners, some fit the image of a color gang perfectly, some were housewives— Some were— Some were— Some were—

That was the group collected in this scene. Many of them were on the younger side, to be certain, but from a distance it looked like nothing more extraordinary than a larger than usual crowd for this time of night.

Even the police could easily be fooled if called. That was exactly the point of the group, and thus it melted into the town without suspicion.

Until a single e-mail reached the entire group.

*   *   *

Mikado waited for the right moment and sent a preprepared message to essentially every member of the group with a mail address on their cell phone, all at once.

"Right now anyone not looking at messages on their phones is an enemy. Do not attack, just stare silently."

♂♀

Namie and her goons were instantly singled out in the crowd, overwhelmingly outnumbered.

A single dullahan observed the scene from far above. She had to determine who was an enemy and who was a friend.

The ones who still brandished weapons in the midst of the stares, taking positions to protect Namie. They were the enemy to her and to the Dollars.

In exchange for her help with the plan, Celty got to meet the girl with her head earlier in the evening. She approached the girl, neck covered in gruesome stitched scars, and simply asked for her name. It was a fatalistic question—she assumed the girl would not remember—but the answer was the worst thing she could have imagined.

The girl stared at Celty's helmet with awful, empty eyes and said just one word.

"Celty."

That cleared my head.

As soon as the word registed in her mind, she felt a deep despair, as well as the invigorating rush of being set free of some kind of curse.

Celty gazed down on Namie's squad, isolated from the enormous crowd—and announced her presence by letting her Coiste Bodhar roar.

All at once, the crowd of Dollars looked away from Namie and up at Celty on the top of a looming high-rise building.

Satisfied, she spread her arms—

And dropped vertically down the outer surface of the building.

Before the screams started down on the ground, the shadow that enveloped her expanded to its maximum, an even blacker cloud against the black of night. The shadow eventually covered the bike, weaving its way between the tires and the wall so that both rubber and steel seemed to draw the other in as it raced breathless and vertical.

The Dollars and Namie's group, gathered below on 60-Kai Street, were getting a glimpse of a world where physics held no sway.

The bike leaped away from the building and landed on the opposite side of the Dollars, trapping Namie's group in the middle.

It was like a scene from a movie. Some held their breath, some quaked in terror, and some shed tears without knowing why.

And without a care for the public attention on her every move, Celty drew the shadow from her back, forming the giant pitch-black scythe.

As Namie trembled, one of her henchmen approached Celty from behind and smacked her collarbone area with a special police baton. The helmet fell off of her neck, exposing the empty space.

Shouts and screams arose, while those at the rear of the pack couldn't see or react to what happened. Panic shot through the crowd.

But Celty had not an ounce of doubt or hesitation.

Yeah, I have no head. I'm a monster. I don't have a mouth to speak my case or eyes to convey my passion to others.

But so what?

So damn what?

I'm right here. I am here, and I exist. If I don't have any eyes, you will simply have to observe all of my actions instead. Let your ears take in the screams of those who have felt firsthand my monstrous wrath.

I am right here. I'm here. I'm right here.

I am already screaming, screaming.

I was born here—so that I could carve my existence into this city...

And then, they *heard*. The sight turned into a tremendous noise in their brains.

The scream of the dullahan, a sound they should never have heard, painted the main street in the color of battle.

Last
Chapter
Dollars, Closing

At first, the Dollars were nothing more than a silly idea.

On Mikado's suggestion, a number of friends on the Internet decided to work together. They created a fictional team in Ikebukuro and spread the tales solely on the Net. They added story upon story, claiming Dollars' responsibility for any real event that happened. None of them ever claimed to be a member of the Dollars but spoke of them as tales they heard from others. When people asked for the source of the information, they were ignored. Sometimes the group even set up fake websites to back their claims.

When the tale of the Dollars began to gain legs of its own, Mikado and his friends got a little carried away and created an official Dollars site. It was password protected, and they wrote a huge mass of "member posts" within. Then they began to leak the address—if anyone wanted the password, they'd send it along in an e-mail, claiming they got it on the down low from a friend within the group.

In this way, they created a fake organization. The only rule was listed on the website: "You are free to claim membership in the team."

Of course, at first people claimed there was no such team in Ikebukuro. But strangely enough, over time posts appeared that called out such opinions as the work of trolls or accused them of never having been to Ikebukuro in the first place. None of Mikado's original group were making these posts. In other words, people who weren't in on the original joke were speaking up to defend the Dollars.

At first, they were delighted over this development, but that soon gave way to subtle unease and chilling alienation.

Yes, it was a silly joke at first. They intended to put work into building up the story, then let it sit, like a little prank. But then things started getting weird.

The Dollars, which had begun as an empty prank, began to wield actual real-world strength.

Whose work it was did not surface, but gradually, people began to join the Dollars in real life, through face-to-face communication, not on the Internet. The story was growing larger and larger beyond their control. At that point, they didn't have the option of coming out and claiming it was all a big joke, and Mikado's friends began to drift away from it. They preferred to simply fade away and forget about the whole thing.

Only Mikado kept up the act.

Now that the organization actually had true power, someone had to take control, to ensure it was safe. He couldn't deny that a part of him was elated over the illusion that he was in control of such a massive group, but he kept it entirely secret—and the next thing he knew, he was in fact the head of the Dollars.

The leader atop the Dollars, a person no one had ever seen, a person no one would have guessed was only in middle school. And the group only picked up speed from there.

Finally, tonight, the organization born from a lie took on absolute substance.

"Boy, that was something," Izaya muttered, watching the aftermath of the festival.

In less than three minutes, Celty crushed ten men, then disappeared in pursuit of the fleeing Namie.

The crowd seemed to treat the entire display as an illusion, breaking off into smaller groups and continuing on their ways home. It was like the draining of some tremendous tide, and the mob was gone as though it had all been nothing more than the product of a dream.

All that was left was a few cars parked on the street and the same old night bustle that had been in place before the event.

"Were there really *that* many people here just now?" Kadota asked Izaya Orihara as he got out of one of the vans on the street. He hadn't seen Izaya in ages.

"Nice to see you again, Dotachin. For the number of people they hold, the twenty-three wards of Tokyo are surprisingly small. It's the densest city in the world for a reason. You can show up anywhere and disappear anywhere."

As they chatted, Celty appeared at the entrance to the street nearby.

"By the way, Izaya...what is that? I've seen it before. It's not human, is it?"

"You saw it, right? It's a monster. Make sure you call it that out of respect," Izaya joked, then walked over toward Celty. "Seems like you lost your target, huh?"

His tone was as casual toward her as ever, despite having just witnessed the majesty of her combat in person. Celty trudged back to her motorcycle in fatigue, clearly upset about losing Namie.

"Well, at least you cleared your head," he noted cheerfully, looking straight at the cross section of neck remaining.

Damn. So he knew I didn't have my head all along.

Izaya was cool as a cucumber even without Celty's head present. Meanwhile, Yumasaki and Karisawa were still positively buzzing with excitement, chattering a slight distance away.

"No way, no way, you serious? Is this for real? It's not just my eyes playing tricks on me? Wait, does that mean the Black Rider's all CG or something?!"

Celty grew tired of their stares, so she walked over to pick up her fallen helmet.

"The thing that makes ghosts scary is that they skulk and hide around before popping out to spook you. But after that grand entrance back there, nobody around here's going to be afraid of you for quite a while," Izaya teased her, then added, "And you didn't even kill anyone, huh? Can't your scythe cut anything?"

She ignored him completely and brushed the dust off of her helmet. The scythe she'd produced just now was fashioned to be safe on either edge. If anything, it was more of a bludgeon.

If I'm planning to live in this place for a while, it won't do to make the town infamous for murders.

But she wasn't going to admit such a shabby reasoning to anyone. She slouched her shoulders in embarrassment and put the helmet back on top.

♂♀

Before they parted, Izaya approached Mikado.

"To be honest, I'm amazed," he said pleasantly, but there was not a drop of sweat on his face to support that statement. Mikado couldn't begin to guess where he had been in the crowd.

Meanwhile, Izaya praised the young man. "I knew there were a ton of people identifying themselves as Dollars on the Net. But I never thought you could call a meeting out of the blue like this and get so many people all at once. Ahh, humanity always surpasses one's imagination."

He shook his head softly. "But while you may be dreaming of a life outside the bounds of normality, life in Tokyo will become normal after you've been here for a year. If you still want the abnormal, you'll need to either move somewhere else or get into drugs, prostitution, or whatever lies even deeper underground."

At that point, Mikado understood. If he did the same thing again, seeking the same high of excitement he was now feeling—or perhaps if he publicly and completely claimed leadership of the Dollars—what would become of him? If he was unhappy with his life now, would he just keep searching for a new life forever?

Izaya smiled in absolute understanding of Mikado's thoughts.

"Life becomes normal even for the people on the other side of the tracks. Take the plunge for yourself, and you'll be used to it in three days. And people like you can never bear that."

It was painful how well he understood what Izaya meant. But why was he saying these things to Mikado? There had to be some ulterior motive, but Mikado had no answer while he was ignorant of Izaya's true intentions.

"If you truly want to escape the ordinary, you'll simply need to keep evolving—whether what you seek is above or below."

To finish off, he patted Mikado's shoulder and said, "Enjoy your normality. Out of respect, I'll let you have Namie Yagiri's phone number absolutely free. And I'll even refrain from selling the intel that you're the founder of the Dollars. It's your organization. Use it when you want to use it."

And with that, he walked off in Celty's direction. Mikado wasn't quite sure how to process all of this, so he simply bowed toward Izaya's back.

However, Izaya suddenly stopped and turned back, adding one last thing that had just come to him.

"Just so you know, I've been observing you on the Net this entire time. I just wanted to catch a glimpse of the guy who actually created something as dumb as the Dollars. That's all! Hang in there, *Tarou Tanaka!*"

But how did he know that name, something Mikado had chosen as a username exclusively for certain areas online? And on a similar note, hadn't he called Kadota "Dotachin" just a few moments earlier?

He thought back to what Izaya had just said—he was observing the creator of the Dollars on the Net, tracking his online behavior.

Then Mikado remembered one of his chat partners, a person who had invited him to a specific chat room, and claimed to know various things about Ikebukuro and the Dollars.

Can it be? Can it be? Can it be?!

♂♀

Eventually, the police came to sweep 60-Kai Street, but Mikado in his school jacket hid in the shadows of an alleyway with Celty. If the police found him wearing proof that he was in school, he'd be punished for certain.

The passersby and karaoke bar solicitors unrelated to the Dollars no doubt witnessed the raucous scene from earlier, but no one spoke up to tell the police what happened. Either they decided that nothing so freaky was a good idea to get involved with, or they assumed they'd hallucinated the entire thing.

But for some reason, even after the police had left, the unease sat heavy in Mikado's heart. He felt that he must be forgetting something important. Meanwhile, Celty, her helmet back on her shoulders, walked over to the van in which her head was sitting.

She no longer held any longing for her head, but it seemed appropriate that she say a final farewell of some kind. But as she approached the van—

Shudd.

A dull shock ran through her back as she reached for the car door. A moment later, the sensation repeated, slightly higher.

Huh? Isn't this the same thing that happened to Shizuo yesterday...?

The shock instantly turned to pain, and Celty fell to her knees. She looked behind her to see a tall young man wearing a school jacket. There was a large scalpel in his hand, probably taken from a laboratory.

After a brief silence, enough time for the wounds to heal and the pain to fade, the boy mumbled, "Hmm, I guess that's not enough to kill."

Seiji Yagiri examined the blade, noting there was no blood on it, then hopped right into the van.

Wait, where are you going?

Celty instantly forgot about being stabbed in the back. She wasn't sure how to handle this unexpected arrival. As far as she could remember, this was Yagiri, who'd been chasing her head—the younger brother of the woman from earlier. As with the time that he stabbed Shizuo, she was struck by how *normal* he was, and that made it all the harder to know how to respond.

Seiji Yagiri stepped into the van without hesitation and boldly carried his heroine out.

"Huh...?"

At a distance, Mikado had to squint to see what happened.

He thought he saw a man wearing a blazer get into the van, and then just moments later, he got right back out, pulling with him a girl with scars on her neck.

Seiji had a dazzling smile on his face as he pulled her by the hand. With a powerful look in his eye, he led her away from the van.

No one, not Karisawa in the car, or Celty nearby, tried to stop him. No one could.

His actions inside the van were too simple and too bold. At first, Karisawa took him for one of Mikado's friends. He was wearing the same uniform, and there was no hesitation or doubt in his eyes.

And with that pure look of devotion on his face, he reached out a hand to the scarred girl.

"I've come for you. Let's go."

If that was all that happened, Karisawa or Celty could have stopped him. But the next moment took them completely by surprise.

"...Okay."

The girl with the scarred neck took Seiji's hand without a second thought. As though he completely expected this answer, he nodded and pulled her out of the vehicle. It happened so naturally, it was as though fate had ordained that moment from before they were ever born. The glowing night street was like their wedding aisle.

"Huh? What?"

Despite his bewilderment, Mikado couldn't take his eyes off of the unnatural scene.

Kadota and Yumasaki, too, seemed to think that Seiji was Mikado's friend, given the same school uniform, and they watched him go without much consternation. Izaya, on the other hand, did understand the meaning of the events, but he was content to watch the scene play out with a smile on his lips.

Eventually Seiji noticed Mikado on the street, and he approached with the girl in tow.

"Hey."

The greeting was so ordinary—and therefore eerie, given the circumstances—that Mikado had no response. Seiji continued, not bothered in the least.

"I really owe a lot to both you and my sister. If it wasn't for my sister, I'd never have found her. And if it wasn't for you, she'd have been trapped in that lab forever."

And with that, he walked right past Mikado. The boy watched them pass with shock, but then he noticed the expression on the face of the girl. She averted her eyes, but he thought he caught a hint of fear.

Mikado glared at Seiji and asked a very important question.

"I'd like you to answer something for me. I tried to get an answer out of your sister earlier…"

"Asking if I had killed someone? It might have happened."

Mikado felt a slight chill run down his back. Seiji did not change his expression. He pointed the scalpel right at Mikado, who stood in his way.

"Now move it. If it's gotten out that I killed that stalker chick, me and my lady here have to run for safety before the police show up to haul me in."

Seiji's eyes were not filled with madness, nor transported with the lust of violence.

"But that doesn't mean—"

"What do you know? I've been watching her, gazing at her, ever since I was a little kid. I wanted to release her, free her from the prison of that cramped glass case. I wanted to live with her out in the free world. That's all I ever, ever, ever, ever, ever, ever thought about."

His eyes were never anything but normal and full of justified intent. This must have been the "ordinary life" that he chose for himself, but from the outside, it was impenetrable and terrifying.

"Hey, what are you doing?"

Izaya, Kadota, Yumasaki, and the others noticed the scene unfolding and gathered around them. Seiji simply stood his ground and shook his head.

"Oh, come on. The power of love cannot be stopped by anyone."

Even surrounded by menacing figures, his expression was absolutely ordinary. He spun the scalpel and held it high, then turned to Mikado and shouted, "So what does that make you? Both then *and* now, you rely on simple numbers and make no extraordinary effort of your own. You're like a third-rate villain. I bet you've never been in love."

"And you can't even be third-rate if you don't understand the effort it takes to gather these numbers," Mikado replied.

Seiji smirked and swung the scalpel down. At the same time, a black shadow raced up from behind and struck his body.

"—!"

Celty had been waiting for the right moment and smacked his hand with the butt of her scythe to knock the scalpel loose, but despite the incredible pain in his wrist, he did not drop it. Instead, he swung at Mikado again from his bent position.

"My love will not be broken by the likes of this," he claimed, trying to pull the girl along despite the odds against him.

Seiji gripped the knife and swiped sideways in a huge arc, trying to force everyone in front of him to back away. Celty quickly struck him again, but—

"That won't work on me."

"Dude, is this guy *on* something?" Kadota wondered aloud. Seiji's expression was as strong and forthright as ever, without an ounce of pain or hesitation.

"It won't work! I feel pain—I just shake it off! Me and Celty don't need pain in our life together! So anything you do to me, I refuse to feel as pain!"

"You're acting crazy!" Mikado shouted. Celty raised her scythe and prepared to cut the tendons in Seiji's arm.

What is wrong with him? He needs to be stopped. Is this...the form his love takes? What in the world are his values? Does this mean that my views and humans' are entirely different? I have, I have my own, my own, my own—

She swung the scythe in a tight arc, as much to drive away her own thoughts as anything else. Somehow, the double-sided bluntness of the scythe had given way to a razor-sharp edge. Noting this, Mikado and the other human beings in the vicinity took a wide step backward.

Just as Celty's scythe was about to descend upon Seiji's arm...

"Stooooop!"

Everyone went still.

Except for two: Seiji and the girl.

The girl with the scars on her neck was standing boldly in the path of the scythe—and seeing this, Seiji tried to shove himself in front of her. The blade of the scythe stopped just before it touched his body, hurting no one.

Meanwhile, everyone stared at the girl in shock.

The "head girl," who called herself Celty, had leaped in the path of harm to save Seiji. Her attitude had changed 180 degrees from her previously quiet and reserved self. She boldly spoke out in Seiji's defense.

"Stop it! Seiji might be harsh and violent and a little different from other people, but he saved my life! He saved me and Anri, but even then, he's already in love with someone else, you see, so…you can't kill him…"

Her voice trembled and lost steam until she fell over onto Seiji in a tearful mess.

No way—no way, no way—
And the dullahan realized:
No…this girl is not my head.

At the exact same moment, Mikado realized who she was.
She's not the dullahan's head! Her name is—

"Mika…Harima?" he mumbled. She turned trembling eyes on him. "It's true, isn't it? You're Mika Harima, who was supposedly killed by Seiji, aren't you?"

"That's a lie," said Seiji. The instant he heard her voice and name, the memories had begun flooding back into his mind. The stalker who looked so much like his beloved. The girl he had killed by smashing her head into the wall… "It's not true, is it?"

"…I'm sorry! I'm sorry, I…I'm sorry…"

"I actually…wasn't completely dead! I clung to life…and your sister asked…if I wanted you to fall in love with me! And even though you almost killed me, I still loved you so much… And then a doctor showed up…and said with a bit of surgery and the right makeup…I could look just like that head…the head that Seiji loves so much!"

Celty's body twitched.

"But then...the doctor said, 'Your name is Celty. That's the head's name.' And I decided to try to be Celty for Seiji's sake...but Namie said it wasn't working, that I wouldn't be able to fool him... She was going to erase my memory with surgery or drugs! But...I didn't want to forget my love for him... I just wanted to tell him how I felt...so I escaped the lab!"

Seiji's sister must have wanted to combine the head with a living human being so she could try to pry him away from it. But only Namie truly knew if that was to make him a normal human being again or if it was out of jealousy toward the head.

Various pieces were connecting together in Celty's mind to form a complete picture.

There were only so many people who knew her name. And out of them, the only one who knew she was a dullahan was—

Shinra Kishitani. Celty's living partner, the underground doctor who knew her secret.

Thinking back further, Celty remembered when she had considered seeking hints on the head's whereabouts through the research labs of medical manufacturers or universities. But Shinra himself volunteered for that job, saying, "I know people in Yagiri Pharmaceuticals, so I can check on my own. It would be silly to owe Orihara a favor for something like this."

He came back saying that nothing seemed suspicious or out of place—but looking back on it now, he must have known that the head was at Yagiri Pharmaceuticals all along and volunteered for the fact-finding mission to hide that from her...

She clenched her fists, all interest lost in Mika or Seiji, and bowed briefly to Mikado before hopping on her bike. The roar of the engine burst through the black of night.

It was its fiercest screech all evening, signaling the conclusion of the night's festivities.

"No way... This can't... I...I never...noticed?"

An evil shadow loomed closer to plant the final blow on Seiji's defenseless back.

"Well, well. Looks like you couldn't even tell the difference between the real thing and a counterfeit. I mean, if we're being honest, that just shows you how real your love for that head is. Nice work, pal," Izaya crowed.

Seiji's heart crumbled to pieces. He fell to his knees.

"Seiji!"

His classmate raced to his side, stitching scars around her neck—Mika Harima.

From Mikado's perspective, it was all an absurd comedy of errors, but for some reason, he couldn't bring himself to laugh about it. He thought for a moment, then approached and shyly spoke to the two.

"Umm…maybe you didn't realize that she was an impostor, but you still risked your life to save hers. I think that's really incredible," he said, trying to cheer up Seiji, then turned to Mika. "And after I heard your side of the story, I realized that I was wrong about you. True, you've got some…character flaws…but you're not a stalker."

When he spoke again, it was more to himself than anything. "Then again…it's probably about as bad. I think it's a possessive urge that drives stalking behavior. But she put her life on the line for Yagiri's sake. I don't think you could do something like that if it was solely out of a selfish desire. Plus, the fact that she still loves the guy who almost killed her is pretty astonishing…in a variety of ways."

And with one last unnecessary comment, Mikado left to join the night.

"I think you two are very, very similar."

♂♀

Near Kawagoe Highway, top floor of an apartment building, late night

The instant she turned the key in the lock, Celty kicked in the door of Shinra's apartment.

"Oh, welcome home."

Shinra greeted her with his usual smile, sitting in the living room at his computer. Celty did not bother to undo her shadow boots. She strode directly over to the young man in his white lab coat and grabbed him by the collar.

She wasn't in the mood to punch at a keyboard, but punching him wouldn't be enough, either. She considered how best to register her anger with him.

"Let me guess: 'What are you playing at?'" he said, putting words to her emotions. "Next you're going to say, 'You knew! You knew my head was in that lab for the last twenty years! You and your father have been working with Yagiri Pharmaceuticals from the start! Now that I think back on it, when you two first laid eyes on me, you seemed too calm and accepting! Could it be that your father is the one who stole my head in the first place?! And then you chose to hide the truth, found work as a black market doctor, and mocked up a half-dead girl to look like me! I might be a monster, but you're the *true* monster here!' Does that cover it?"

"…!!"

"Oh, and just to clear up any confusion…I don't know if my dad is the one who stole your head, and I don't really care either way. Plus, that plastic surgery was done at the girl's request. Perhaps the Yagiri people prodded her into doing it, but that's no concern of mine."

At last, Celty let her grip on his collar loosen the slightest bit. Her trembling fists fell still, stopped in time.

If I could speak aloud, I suppose I would have said each and every one of the words he just attributed to me.

"Let me guess, 'Can you tell what I'm thinking?' I didn't think it even needed to be said."

He didn't need to wait for her answer. He knew what her answer would be.

"Yes, I can. I've loved you for twenty years. Of course I can tell that much."

"…"

"If you ask me, people place far too much emphasis on the face when reading the emotions of others. Slight differences in the tension of muscles or the sound of footsteps can tell all you need to know to instantly sense how another person is feeling. And I've been watching you do this for years."

Then why? Why would you keep quiet about the whereabouts of my head until now?

He saw right through her mind, and his voice was heavy with intent and emotion.

"Because I love you. That's why I stayed quiet about your head."

"...?"

"Once you got your hands on it, you'd have been gone. I couldn't stand that happening."

In short, he was confessing his own selfishness, but there was an optimistic shine to his words.

"I'm not going to say that I'll give up if that's truly what will make you happy. This is a battle of your love against mine. Remember what I said? I will spare no effort in seizing victory in our game of fate. So that poor girl—Mika, her name was? I used her in an attempt to make you give up on your head. I'm not going to let you go. I will use the love of others, their deaths, my own self, even your own emotions to keep you here—as contradictory as that sounds."

In a way, his words were extremely twisted and insane, but there was no doubt clouding his eyes. That was what broke Celty's will. If he'd played dumb or given her some lame excuse, she would have beaten him until he couldn't stand and left, never to return. But after such a strong, direct statement of intent, Celty had no response.

She lowered Shinra to the ground again and tapped on the keyboard, trying to regain the sharpness of her anger.

"I'm not going to leave you just because I get my head back—"

"That might be your desire—but it might not be your head's," he answered gravely, without any of his usual playfulness. "I've given it a good deal of thought. Why is it that in this wide, wide world, you're the only one who has shown herself to mankind? What is the boundary that separates you from the rest of the dullahans? I think it's your head. Perhaps losing your head was what allowed you to materialize in our world—made you what you are now."

He took on a fateful, lovelorn expression, as though reciting a tragic monologue he'd written.

"What if you get your head back and regain your memory, and then you disappear like mist in the morning sun, as though your entire existence until now had been nothing but a hallucination? That thought terrifies me."

Celty gently lowered herself onto a nearby chair and sat still for several moments.

The sound of the keyboard echoed off the walls of the still room.

"Do you believe what I tell you?"

"I trust you. In fact, I don't trust anything *but* you."

Satisfied, Celty slowly typed out a confession of her own.

"I'm scared, too."

"I'm scared of dying."

"I know that I am invincible. I understand it as a simple truth that there is not a human being in the world who can kill me. That is not a boast but pure fact. I register no joy or emotion in this fact. But that's what is so scary. As I am now, there is no part of my body that is in charge of my death. There's only one explanation: that my head is that part. Somebody could destroy my head without me even being there. And completely isolated from my own will or circumstances, I would..."

She stopped typing there, paused for a moment, then continued tapping the keys.

"Would you believe me? I have no eyes or brain, but I dream. Would you believe that I tremble in fear of this nightmare? It's this fear, the selfish desire to control my own death, that leads me to search for my head. If I told you that, would you believe me?"

Shinra read every single letter of the confession as it appeared on the screen. When she stopped typing at last, he answered instantly.

"I told you—I don't believe in anything *but* you."

And with that, he smiled happily. Smiled like he was about to cry.

"I am utterly and truly lost. I guess we've both been stubborn, working off of nothing but assumptions."

"So stupid."

The dullahan slowly got to her feet and leaned over to type with one hand.

"Hey, Shinra."

"What?"

"Let me punch you."

"Sure," he replied without missing a beat—and just as quickly, Celty put her fist through his face.

The tremendous sound of the impact echoed off the walls, and the man in his white coat sprawled across the floor. Blood streamed from his mouth, and he lay prone for several moments. Eventually he got back up and faced Celty again.

"Then let me return the favor."

Celty had done nothing to deserve being hit back, but she nodded her assent anyway.

As soon as he saw the empty helmet tilt forward, Shinra swung a powerless fist and knocked it off.

Her helmet clattered and spun on the floor.

—?

She had no immediate response to that meaningless, confusing action. The doctor grinned and rubbed his smarting hand.

"There, see? You're at your most beautiful in your natural state, Celty," he said, staring at the empty space over her neck. "That punch was our version of a promise kiss."

She hunched her shoulders down and leaned into his chest—so she could deliver a sharp jab to his gut.

"*Bhurgh!*"

But she stayed where she was, leaning against his chest.

Meanwhile, her left hand typed, "*You're such an idiot.*"

There was no need for words anymore. Shinra held her close in silence.

The little shivers that wracked her slender frame told him that she was crying.

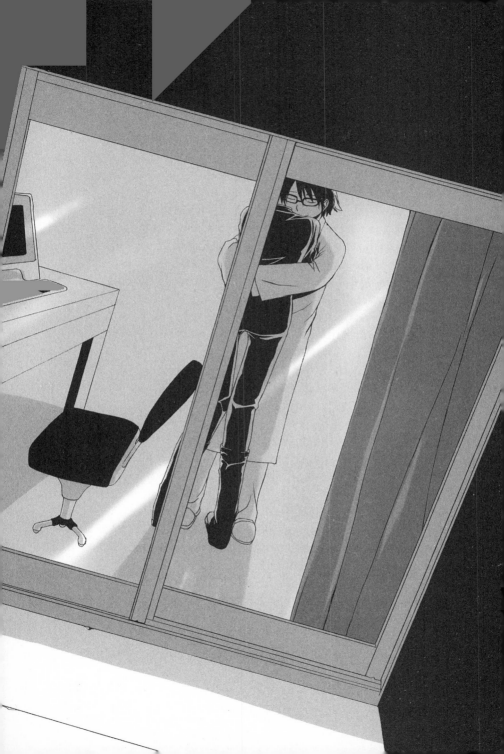

♂♀

Shinjuku, early morning

It was all for her brother's sake.

Actually, there was no benefit for Seiji—it was entirely for the sake of her desire to see him smile—but she had no personal awareness of this fact.

Immediately following the scene on 60-Kai Street, Namie Yagiri took the head out of the lab. As she expected, shortly after she left there came a report that the Black Rider—the dullahan's body—had rushed the lab. But she already had the head. If the dullahan got its head back, either Seiji would fall into the depths of despair, or he'd claim that his fated lover was finally whole again for him.

Neither of those options Namie wanted to see.

She had to control the head at all times. It was the only hope she had to keep her brother's attention on her.

But when she called her uncle hoping to employ his help, she received news that she certainly wasn't expecting to hear.

There had been an emergency meeting of senior management to confirm the merger with Nebula. Both the company and Nebula must have been observing the incidents surrounding the research lab, not just tonight, but the last several days. Whichever side suggested it, the intention was clearly to finish the deal before any more nonsense occurred.

Naturally, Nebula wanted the dullahan's head.

Namie slammed the phone down and had the driver turn the car around. She swore never to return to the company and headed off for a group that could help her hide the head.

She couldn't expect help from the mob; they didn't have any use for a head like that. If she brought it to another lab, they might prioritize her treatment while they needed her data, but eventually she would be removed from control.

Pushed to the brink of despair, she turned to one last person.

"This is the first time we've met in person. Did that list of illegal immigrants help meet your experiments' needs?"

She was standing in the apartment of Izaya Orihara.

"But then you had to be stupid and screw it all up. You ruined every-thing thanks to your brother's twisted love—or was it *your* twisted love for your brother?" Izaya wondered, placing an Othello piece on the board. He was speaking to Namie, who sat directly across from him, but his eyes never left the game board.

"Your superiors aren't going to like this, are they? Nebula's a major foreign corporation—hell, they're a mega-conglomerate. They push people around over in the United States."

He placed another Othello piece, trapping a shogi pawn between two black pieces.

"And this piece is promoted."

He flipped the pawn over, turning it into a king. To anyone else, it was a baffling sight, but it clearly meant something to him.

"Kinda dangerous for you, isn't it? What if they send the mafia after you? Perhaps a crack sniper, hired through a Swiss bank, to put a bul-let through your eyes, *blam!* And check."

He slid the king one space forward, placing the other king in check.

"Why can't there be a rule that kings can capture each other?"

For the first time, Izaya looked up at Namie. Her eyes were empty with anxiety and irritation—she was in no mood for his games.

He opened the special case sitting next to the shogi board and stared at the head inside. Then he turned to Namie and began to propound an odd theory.

"I think your uncle was a lot like me. He believed in the afterlife less than anyone else. He feared death more than anyone else. And he craved heaven more than anyone else."

Namie tried to imagine her uncle's face in Izaya, hoping for some insight into his personality, but she had a shocking lack of interest for any member of her family other than Seiji, and in the moment she could barely remember what her uncle was like.

"But he found the truth. And so did I. There *is* another world beyond ours. Let's just leave it at that."

"…?"

He ran his fingers gently through the hair of Celty's beautiful head.

"It's said that dullahans only come in what is essentially a female form. Do you know why?"

"...No. My people did some research on mythology, but I thought it was pointless."

"You're too logical and pragmatic for that. But I digress... There are many commonalities and connections between mythological tales found all around the world. There's a heaven called Valhalla in Norse mythology—technically it's not a heaven, but whatever. It's similar to the inn of the afterlife as found in Celtic mythology. The Norse believed in female angels clad in armor called Valkyries who came to escort the souls of mighty, worthy warriors to Valhalla. A woman in armor who comes for the dead—sound familiar?"

What's your point?

Namie had no idea what Izaya was trying to say, but she couldn't help but be concerned by the angular smile that stayed plastered on his face, looking more like a mask with every passing moment.

"According to one theory, a dullahan is just a Valkyrie wandering the earth. That's why the dullahans are only female and often depicted wearing armor. That must mean this head is waiting—waiting for the awakening. For the battle. Searching for the holy warrior to take to Valhalla."

This was entirely his own interpretation, but the way he spoke made it sound like the truth.

"The reason this head's eyes won't open, even though it's alive, is because there's no war here. I wish I could be chosen as her warrior. But I don't have the skills to survive if I took it to the Middle East, let's say."

And with a glint of hope in his voice, his smile shut out everything else.

"If there really is a Valhalla after death, what should I do? A war—I need to start a war myself. But I'm not going to be of any use in the Middle East. So I need to start a war that only I can orchestrate and star in. Isn't that right?"

He placed a finger on the corner of the board covered with Othello, shogi, and chess pieces and spun it with evident pleasure. The pieces scattered and flew, leaving only the promoted pawn still sitting in the center.

"However, if I start a war here in Tokyo, one that involves no armies or governments, I'm positive that I have what it takes to survive. How lucky I am! I lived without faith in heaven, lived a life far from holiness—and because of that, I met a fallen angel of death here on earth!"

Izaya grinned with unbridled glee, his smile devoid of expression. There was no room for anyone or anything to affect his excitement. Namie opened her mouth to say something, but could only produce the clumsiest rebuttal.

"That's just, like...your opinion."

"There is only salvation for those of faith. Besides, I'm just saying, this is insurance. I'm taking out insurance on the afterlife. Maybe it's hell—a place with nothing but suffering—but at least I'll exist there. Still, if I have the option, I'd prefer heaven."

He called out to her like he was asking her out to dinner. "Hey, Namie, let's all go to heaven together."

As she looked at his mask of pleasure, Namie realized that she was giving this "agent of heaven" to the very last person on earth that she should. He smiled at her.

"I'll take custody of this head as a member of the Dollars. Celty would never imagine that her head was under her team's own control, would she?"

Dollars? Celty's team?

The unfamiliar information closed in on Namie's will, bewildering her. Izaya giddily offered a deal with the devil.

"You should join the Dollars yourself. Our boss has a policy of pulling in anyone and everyone who comes to us. Of course, *I'm* the one who really started recruiting people."

He seemed to belittle her, care for her, and bless her all at once.

"Let's help our fallen angel find her wings and take flight again, shall we?"

♂♀

South Ikebukuro Park, early morning

This is a twisted story.

"I do not love you."
A man and woman were leaning against each other on a park bench under the brightening sky.
"But as long as you're around, I won't forget my love and dedication for her. Therefore, I accept your love. At least, until the day I get her back," Seiji said in an empty voice as he softly embraced Mika's body.
Mika smiled to herself. There was a quiet conviction in that smile.
I have to be that head for Seiji to truly love me. Therefore, I will sacrifice everything I have to love him. I'll do anything I can to help him find that head. And when we do, I'll grind it to a pulp right in front of him, pour the remains into my mouth, and make it part of my flesh and blood. It's all for his sake, for his sake, for his sake...

A love between them that would last until the moment their true love came true.
A love that was so straightforward and so terribly twisted.
The sight of them was so delicate and precious—and so horribly, horribly wrong.

Like a grade-schooler on the day after watching the latest episode of the hottest anime, Masaomi's face was plastered with an enormous grin.

"Mikado, you won't believe what I saw on the Net... Get this, there was a Dollars meetup yesterday! Turns out Simon and Shizuo are both in the Dollars! And the Black Rider showed up totally headless and swinging a scythe and went like *vwoww!* right down the wall!"

"I don't understand a word of what you just said."

School hadn't vanished off the map, even following a night like the one before. The clock on the wall ticked away the seconds as though nothing had ever happened, and a perfectly boring, normal day passed by.

When the lunch period began, Mikado headed for the roof of the main school building. Nearly everyone else went to the school cafeteria, which was as large and deluxe as those on a university campus—or else they ventured out into the nearby neighborhood to order a quick lunch. Only a few weird students who brought home-cooked lunches bothered to eat up on the roof.

Mikado stared up at the sky, the same sight as it was anywhere else in town, and had the utterly ordinary epiphany that this was the exact same sky he saw back in his hometown. It was strange to think that after such an abnormal experience, he could find such a sense of relief and peace in his heart. It was the peace that came the day after a long-awaited field trip.

The day after the incident, Mikado came to school rubbing sleepy eyes to find Seiji Yagiri sitting in his seat, perfectly matter-of-fact. He did not look at Mikado during class, but when their first break started, he turned and briefly said, "Sorry for everything," before returning to his seat.

More surprising was Mika Harima's sudden attendance. Anri was surprised at the slight changes to her face, but since most of the students had never seen her until this day, she didn't strike them as strange in the least, if you ignored the bandage around her neck.

Mika gave Mikado a brief word of thanks from the seat next to him. When the break started, she immediately started clinging to Seiji.

"Damn, so *that's* Seiji's girlfriend? No way! No wonder he lives in love, then!" Masaomi remarked. Mikado put on an uncomfortable smile—he knew more of the truth than his friend did—and muttered an affirmative.

But it seemed that after the latest turn of events, Mika no longer hung out with Anri. Each time they had a break between periods, Anri sat alone in the corner of the classroom. Mikado watched her, feeling conflicted.

Whether or not this was a good thing for her was something that only she knew. But...was that really true? Was there no way for him to understand? Perhaps no one really understood the heart of another.

"You'll simply need to keep evolving," echoed Izaya's words in his head.

Fine, then, I will evolve. I'll find out just how much I can evolve within the ordinary world I've been given—and then I'll show it to him.

At this point, he had no idea if it was up or down that he'd been looking all this time. As a matter of fact, whatever the answer, he was still looking that way now. The only difference is that he'd made a little wiggle room for himself, front and back.

Mikado stared out the classroom window at the sixty-story building overhead and reflected on his own feelings.

After his experience with the absolutely unreal and extraordinary, he was left with an odd mixture of fulfillment and emptiness.

I bet now I can stare reality right in the face. I can accept it.

And once he decided that he was ready to be honest with himself, he knew what he needed to do.

Mikado was on the roof. From what he heard, she ate lunch here every day.

After such a bold maneuver, he thought that he was capable of anything. He thought nothing could scare him anymore.

He didn't expect to get tripped up over something like this.

It was so easy to reach out and talk to people on the Internet...

He never in his wildest dreams expected that it would be so hard to achieve his desires in ordinary, real life.

Who knew that it took so much courage just to ask a girl in your class to hang out?

The boy will find Anri in thirty seconds.

The boy will spot Masaomi attempting to woo Anri in thirty-five seconds.

The boy will kick Masaomi to the ground in forty-five seconds.

The boy will suffer Masaomi's rolling sobat kick in fifty seconds.

The boy will ask Anri to a café in seventy-three seconds.

The boy will be rejected by Anri in seventy-four seconds.

The boy will be invited to eat lunch on the roof by Anri in seventy-eight seconds.

The boy will fall in love with Anri in—

The boy will profess his love for Anri in—

Chat room

At the end of the day, Mikado turned on his computer. He was curious how the Internet was reacting to the previous night's events, but it didn't seem to be spreading much. A few people had posted about the dullahan, but no one was taking them seriously.

Figures, Mikado snorted to himself, then took a look in the chat room he visited just about every day—the chat room that Izaya had invited him to, using the nickname Kanra. The only other person in the room was his friend under the name of Setton.

Another person invited to the chat room by Kanra. I wonder if Setton has some secret identity, too...

—TAROU TANAKA HAS ENTERED THE CHAT—
【Good evening.】
[Evening. I've just been waiting around.]
【Okay. I'm pretty tired tonight, so I won't be around for long.】
[Lack of sleep? Did you pull an all-nighter?]
【Kind of.】
[Kanra's not online yet, I guess.]
【Do you suppose he'll show up?】
[Uh-oh. Sorry, something's come up that I need to take care of.]
【Oh, is that so?】
[Sorry, bye.]
【Okay, good night.】
—SETTON HAS LEFT THE CHAT—

"Sorry to interrupt your fun," said the man in the white coat, smiling apologetically.

"*No big deal*," she typed on the keyboard. Celty popped up out of the chair.

"Just be careful—tonight's job could be pretty dicey. Here's the deal..."

She listened to the description of her mission and left the apartment without a sound.

It was the start of another day for Celty.

A black shadow raced down National Route 254.

It was a pitch-black motorcycle without a headlight. Far, far ahead, a number of police cars carved away at the darkness with their red lights.

Ahead of even those patrol cars came the occasional dry blast of an explosion.

When that sound reached the bike, its silent engine roared to life in the night.

♂♀

"Hey, it's the dullahan."

"It's cool and all, but I'm telling you, it's all CG."

Karisawa and Yumasaki chattered happily regarding the rider as she overtook them. They'd seen her true powers at close range, but they didn't seem to appreciate the weight of it all. And it wasn't just them—a startling number of those who witnessed Celty's fight took her completely at face value. Either the sheer force of her presence was so overwhelming that it lost all reality and became a dream to them, or she was simply accepted as a part of the city now.

Some of the witnesses did write about their experiences on the Net, but they were all roundly laughed off as nonsense. Thanks to that response, opinion started to shift to explain that night's meeting itself as just a tall tale, and so the Dollars' profile didn't just explode like it might have. That was probably for the best, seeing as the extra attention would also be coming from the police and yakuza.

However, the events of that night most certainly registered deeply into everyone who was present.

"Why do you suppose he showed up there?" Kadota asked from the front passenger seat without turning around.

"Did you know the Black Rider's actually a member of the Dollars?"

"What? You serious?!"

"I never heard that! So that's why he showed up and went so crazy!"

"Awesome! The Dollars must be, like, invincible by now!"

Kadota closed his eyes as the two in the back chattered away. He thought back to what Izaya had said as he left the scene.

"Dotachin, I just met the boss of the Dollars. Do you know what the team name came from?"

"Like, give us dollars or something?"

"Nope. Basically, the group doesn't do anything. And yet, you continue to sell the name. Nothing more. It's named the Dollars after the adjective *dara-dara*, meaning 'lazy' or 'pointless.' That's all there is to it."

There was no actual structure to the group. The Dollars organization was nothing more than a castle wall—it was the people within that built the kingdom on their own. The rest came down to how big of a facade they could hang outside those walls.

The outside left a name on its own, whether there was anything inside or not. Just like a human being.

Kadota looked at the show playing out ahead of them and grinned wryly to himself.

Just like the Black Rider.

♂♀

The black motorcycle evaded the police by riding on the side of a truck as though it were the street. As the policemen's eyes went wide, a man with a TV camera jabbered away excitedly. He was clearly airing live footage of the chase in progress.

Celty noticed he was there but showed no hesitation in producing a blade from her shadow. It was the largest of any she'd created so far, a giant sickle nearly ten feet across. She swung it back—and howled into the night.

Film me if you want. Expose me if you want. Burn the image of this monster into your minds. But what does it really amount to?

This is my life. The path I've been on for a long time. I have nothing to be ashamed of.

She did not hold her breath in the darkness, but let it shine, exhibiting herself unbound by good or evil.

The ordinary days were devoid of extreme hope or despair. Nothing changing. But overflowing with satisfaction and fulfillment.

As she swung the giant scythe at the black bulletproof vehicle, Celty realized something.

Since the night that she exposed all that she was, everything about the city seemed so much more beloved to her.

Perhaps even more than her missing head...

One of the windows rolled down, and a man inside the car shot at Celty.

The bullet split the helmet and passed inside of it.

In the midst of that empty space—the shadow smiled.

STAFF

Author
Ryohgo Narita

Illustrations & Visual Concepts
Suzuhito Yasuda (AWA Studio)

Design
Yoshihiko Kamabe

Editing
Sue Suzuki

Atsushi Wada

Publishing
ASCII Media Works

Distribution
Kadokawa Shoten

SPECIAL THANKS

Mamizu Arisawa

Masaki Okayu

Takafumi Imada

Erika Nakamura

Gakuto Coda

Soichiro Watase

Members of the Dollars

Durarara!! - The End

CAST

AFTERWORD

Hello. It's nice to meet you—or perhaps, to see you again. I'm Ryohgo Narita.

Thank you very much for picking up my new book, titled *Durarara!!*

It's an extremely strange title, I admit, but if you read the book, you'll understand…perhaps. As I was finishing up writing and revising the manuscript, my editor said, "It's about time for us to submit an official title to marketing," and the first thing I came up with was—

"Du…Durarara?"

My editor said, "Actually, I like how mysterious that is. Let's go with that. But how do you want to handle the English spelling?"

I had no answer because I didn't expect him to accept it. Then, he asked, "Will you throw in an exclamation mark like *Baccano!* or *Bow-wow!* have?"

I still had no answer because I still didn't expect him to accept it. So I said without thinking, "Let's put two on there. Bam-bam!"

After a long silence, I heard the scratching of someone writing on paper, then my editor exploded with laughter on the other side of the phone.

"Bwa-ha-ha-ha-ha! When you write this out, it looks so stupid! **Let's go with that, then!**"

That was the birth of *Durarara!!*—but as for what it means, I'm still not quite sure.

So, as for why I chose the location of Ikebukuro as a setting, it wasn't to piggyback on a popular destination in novels and dramas, but because it's the place I understand most of all.

The depictions of Ikebukuro and Shinjuku in this novel aren't meant to be objective but are wildly fictional, so people who haven't been there, don't believe any of it. And if you have been there, don't just slam the book down and call me a liar, but enjoy it as a work of fiction. The same goes for the depictions of gangs and mobsters. Whew! That should throw off all the people saying, "This guy acts like he knows what he's talking about," "Don't mess with gangsters, man," or "Come see me late night in Ikebukuro, bro."

*   *   *

* Warning: This next part contains spoilers.

This story might be classified as a wild card among the Dengeki Bunko stable. First of all, there's the protagonist who doesn't have a head. I have to thank the editorial staff and my illustrator Mr. Yasuda for putting up with my crazy ideas.

Not only that, but I tried putting in lots of little in-jokes and parodies, some of which are probably way over the top, so I'm expecting to get bashed for it… But all of them are ideas that I found funny, so I'd appreciate it if you oblige me.

All around the world, the headless being trying to find its head is a common trope. There's the story of Sleepy Hollow, which was recently turned into a movie. I think the image of someone without a head has the kind of impact that makes it effective in a horror context. The only thing is, while the knight from that folktale is considered a dullahan by some, it's actually something entirely different.

The topic of a dullahan itself is a very minor one. If you look into more details than what is presented in this book, you'll find that the two-wheeled carriage is made from the bones of the dead and that the root of the dullahan was the Celtic goddess Badb Catha, and so on— but I completely removed any of that mythology. Within *Durarara!!*, Celty is Celty, and any other dullahans are other dullahans.

If the *Durarara!!* series gets to continue, I'd like to take it into even weirder directions. I could have "Dullahan Versus Yellow Scarves Color Gang" or "Dullahan Versus Headhunter"… Then again, I got yelled at just for pitching those ideas.

* Back to my usual procession of appreciation.

To editor-in-chief Suzuki, who always puts up with my nonsense. To my editor Mr. Wada, who is now my double editor.

To the proofreaders who have to deal with my terrible lateness every single time. To the designers who put together the look of the book. To the marketing, publishing, and business arms of Media Works.

To the family, friends, and acquaintances who support me in a variety of ways, especially the people of S. City.

To all the other writers and illustrators in the Dengeki line. Particularly to the people who agreed to lend their likeness to my in-jokes—Mamizu Arisawa, Takafumi Imada, Masaki Okayu, Erika Nakamura—and of course, to Gakuto Coda, who gave me permission to use the in-joke that was furthest out of line.

To Suzuhito Yasuda, who took on the bizarre idea of a headless heroine, came to Tokyo for research, and helped come up with nutty ideas with the editor-in-chief.

And to everyone who decided to read this weird little book, the start of my third series.

To all of the above, with my greatest appreciation—thank you.

From home, February 2004

While watching the trailer for *Zebraman* (directed by Takashi Miike, Sho Aikawa's hundredth leading role) on repeat.

Ryohgo Narita

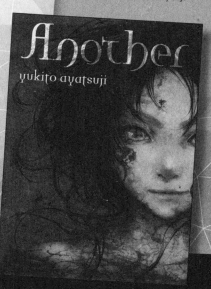

THE BAD, AND THE DOWNRIGHT WEIRD.

The Ikebukuro district in Tokyo is full of interesting people. A boy longing for the extraordinary. A hotheaded punk. An airheaded pseudo-stalker. An information broker who works for kicks. An underground doctor who specializes in truly desperate patients. A high school student infatuated with a monster. And a headless rider on a pitch-black motorcycle. Their story may not be a heartwarming one, but as it turns out, even weirdos like these sometimes fall in love.

US **$14.00**   CAN $16.00

ISBN 978-0-316-30474-0

51400 >

EAN

9 780316 304740

AGES
13 & UP

Visit our website at:
www.yenpress.com

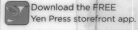
Download the FREE
Yen Press storefront app.

yen
ON

Cover art by Suzuhito Yasuda

Printed in the U.S.A.